THE CONTAINER INCIDENT

THE CONTAINER INCIDENT

Sven Anders Karlberg

MyBooks Publication
A brand of MyBooks Technology Services

Copyright © 2020 Sven Anders Karlberg
[email: s.a.karlberg.author@gmail.com]

First Published in February 2020

by

MyBooks Publication
www.mybookspublication.com

ISBN: 978-93-88282-17-8

Cover Design & Typeset by:
Mybook Technology Services

My sincere gratitude to all who in one way or another contributed to the completion of this book. A special thanks to Sugumaran Kumaran who proof read and did the editorial work.

I dedicated this book to all readers who would read my book and make me stronger and better as a writer.

Table of Contents

About the Author

Sven Anders Karlberg is a professional in International Trade Regulations turned into author. He was born in a small town in the North of Sweden. He studied and worked initially in Sweden. In the later part of his professional journey, he worked and lived in various parts of the world. A super sharp professional who was involved in negotiation of various deals for Trade Compliance regulations not only related to civil commercial applications but also in the government authorities and defense areas for the several countries. He has a special talent of writing from his school days. He is a keen observer which reflects in his writing as well. His writing showcases his special capability of recreating the events.

He is fascinated towards writing thrill stories specifically with international complications which inspired him to write this book.

PART ONE

The Dead Man

Chapter

1

It was an ordinary working day for Kevin Foo, a Chinese male of around sixty years of age. He was close to retirement, but he was not looking forward to it. He lived in a small HDB (Housing Development Board) apartment at Bedok Reservoir Road, block 717. His daily routine was to prepare the breakfast, read the morning newspaper and walk around the Bedok Reservoir before going to work. He had been working at the Criminal Investigation Department in Singapore for more than thirty years.

One of his morning routines was to listen to the National hymn played at the Damai School, close to his apartment. Kevin was still standing in the hallway with his clothes on and his hand on his heart. He stood there listening until the national hymn was played to the end. Then he took his morning walk around the Bedok Reservoir located only across the street where he lived. The morning sun started to shine between the trees and the air was also clear after the heavy rain in the night. After walking a while, he could hear some commotion coming from one of the reservoir's water ditches. The usual view in the morning was to see older men fishing quietly but today it was unusual with high voices and shouting men. The first thing he thought was that somebody had caught a big fish. He increased his speed to get a view of the fish. When he reached the fishing men he could see one of the men was holding his fishing gear straight up in his hands and the other men were pointing into the water and yelling frantically. When Kevin reached the water line, he could clearly see that there was no fish at the end of the line; instead, there was a body of a dead man. Kevin walked right into the water without even taking his new jogging shoes off. He was shouting at the man holding the fishing gear.

"Hey, you. Pull in the line slowly so we can get him a little closer towards the land," Kevin ordered.

The man with the fishing gear started to pull in the dead man as slowly as Kevin had said. The other men were standing and watching. The dead man was now pulled towards the shore and Kevin grabbed one of his legs.

"Call the police and ambulance at once. I will hold the man by his leg until they arrive. I'm a criminal investigator."

One of the fishing men reached for his mobile phone and called the police and the ambulance. After a couple of minutes, they could see the ambulance coming at full speed on the walking path followed by a civil car and a police car with blue lights flashing. The ambulance personnel ran down to the water line together with a civil dressed man. The civil dressed man was one of Kevin's colleagues, Ajay Singh. He was an Indian male, around forty-five years old with a mustache over his lip. Everything he did seemed to be perfect and his self-confidence was high. The main goal for him, now, was to take on bigger cases with high exposure to the public and to be the next Head of the Criminal Investigation Department. The ambulance personnel and the man with fishing gear pulled the body from the water slowly, while Kevin was helping them. Ajay was standing and looking at them while they were pulling out the body from the water. He did not want to ruin his perfect shoe shine.

"What a surprise to see you here, Kevin. I thought you have retired already," Ajay said with a sarcastic tone.

Kevin did not answer Ajay; instead, he helped the ambulance personnel to take the dead man into the ambulance. The ambulance drove away with flashing blue lights. Kevin walked down to the water line to wash his hands and tried to remove the mud from his shoes without any success.

He walked up to Ajay and stood in front of him looking deeply into his eyes. He wanted to make a mark that he did not like Ajay's comment.

"Ajay, you will be the first person to know when I have decided to retire," Kevin said with a smile.

Ajay understood that his comment was not well received by Kevin. Kevin started walking back to his apartment to change the clothes and muddy shoes. Ajay was left standing alone without saying anything.

When Kevin was walking back to his apartment, he started to think about the dead man and the observations he made. He recalled some of the facts that he saw: The age was around forty years, Asian race, long beige Dockers and long-sleeved white shirt, no visible marks on the body, ordinary black shoe on the right foot but on the left foot… there the shoe was missing. This was the only thing that was strange around how he was dressed. Back at the apartment he took a shower, put on new clothes and newly polished shoes. When he was dressed and ready, he called Amanda and informed her that he would be running late to the office.

Amanda Yusof was a Malay descent woman. She worked as the secretary and administrative support for the whole department. Amanda was forty years old and she would wear a hijab to cover her hair, long shirt, and jacket with long sleeves. She was well informed of all the ongoing cases and she always wanted to know where all the investigation officers were at any time.

"Hi, Amanda. I will come to the office later today. I'll explain when I'm back at the office," Kevin said.

"I know what happened this morning. I also heard that Ajay has been appointed to be responsible of that case. You know I think that's the right way, you need to slow down and prepare for the retirement," Amanda said.

Kevin was silent for a long time. He did not like remarks like he should take it easy. He wanted to be on the top of every investigation that he was involved in. He took a deep breath and continued.

"Well, I'm still around and investigating as usual. Nothing has changed."

"Take care now," Amanda said.

Kevin walked quickly from his apartment to the bus stop. He took the bus to Bedok Interchange and then the MRT to the office. Kevin's office at the Criminal Investigation Department had an open plan with work desks placed together in small groups. Only the department's boss had his own office. His office had walls of glass with white curtains to block the view to the inside. Most of the time, the curtains remained open around his office so everybody could see if he was in the office. Everybody in the office also knew that when the curtains were closed there were some serious discussions ongoing inside.

"I'm glad that you are back. There are no emails and no phone calls for you," Amanda said.

Kevin nodded and walked slowly to his desk. His desk was placed opposite to the new young criminal investigator from the Technical Investigation Department. His name was Hamid Munsi and he had started this new position five months ago. He was a young Malay male around thirty years old. He had newly graduated from the police academy with his major in information technology. Hamid was a new type of criminal investigator, intelligent, highly technical competence in several areas. He was casually dressed every day in jeans and a t-shirt with different text messages on it. His desk was easy to recognize with piles and piles of technical computer magazines and other literature, almost science fiction. Kevin had not talked to Hamid so much in the five months they have been sitting close to each other. Kevin was not so interested in Hamid's IS or IT capabilities or what he could offer.

"Hi! Kevin. I heard that you were also down to the reservoir this morning when they picked up the dead man," Hamid said.

"Rumors travel fast in this office. I only happened to be there when the body was found; that's all. Have you heard anything more about that?" Kevin asked.

"Only that Ajay is talking to the autopsy doctor now. I guess you know that Ajay has been assigned this case," Hamid said looking towards Kevin at the same time.

Kevin could feel that he was stared at by all in the office. Kevin did not show any reaction. He continued to read the daily newspaper. About the same time, Amanda walked to Kevin's desk with a serious expression on her face.

"Kevin, the boss wants to talk to you right now," Amanda said.

Kevin's new boss Alex Hen had only been his manager for six months. Alex is around almost fifty years of age and could be described as a Euro Asian. He wore a pair of silver chromed eyeglasses and was the only person wearing a full suit with a jacket in the office. That's the reason why he would force to run the air conditioner at full power and after five minutes in his office, everyone starts freezing. Usually, the people who have the honor to visit his office never stay long in there anyway. He had experience with several high-profile criminal investigations in Singapore, also with Interpol and other International Criminal Institutions. He was appointed here as Head of Criminal Investigation Department, hence Kevin's boss. Kevin kept looking at Amanda for a long time without actually saying anything and then he nodded to Amanda.

"I will take that as an acceptance, but you need to go in there right now. He is waiting for you," Amanda said.

Kevin entered Alex's office without knocking, but he coughed silently to indicate that he was in the room. Alex was reading a file and without even looking up from the document, he just motioned Kevin with his hand to sit down. Alex laid down the document slowly on his desk and smiled at Kevin.

"Kevin, you have a long career in this Criminal Investigation Department and you have served the country well. I can see in this document that you are reaching retirement age soon. Are you looking forward to the retirement?" Alex asked.

"No, not really. Since my wife passed away, I have felt more alone. I have difficulties to find activities I'm interested in," Kevin said.

"That is a known problem for the people who are facing retirement and specifically for those who have successful and active professional careers," Alex said. Kevin nodded as the answer.

Both men were now looking at each other without saying anything. Alex took a deep breath before he continued the discussion.

"I have opened a new position in the department and the position is of a Senior Advisory role for the whole office," Alex said looking at Kevin. He took a pause and then continued. "Kevin, I want you to take this role. We have some young rookies who constantly need advice from an experienced investigator like you. Take Hamid for example; he has never done any field work and you are the person who has done this for thirty years or more. Hamid would be happy to take advice from a senior investigator like you. What do you think?"

Kevin did not show any reaction to Alex's statement. He kept staring out of the window to indicate that he was not so supportive of the proposal. Alex waited silently for him to say something. Kevin now kept his gaze fixed down on to his hands and thinking deeply of the proposal. After a while, Kevin realized that he needed to give Alex an answer.

"This means that I will not have any cases that I can call my own. I guess also that I will not be responsible for anything anymore," Kevin said in a low and depressed voice.

"We are all responsible together for all the cases in this office, Kevin. It's not a one-man show as before. We need to work as a team together with people of different competencies to solve complicated cases. It's not as it was in the old times when one case was for one person. Today, everyone must contribute in all the cases every day and night if the expertise is needed."

"I have heard that Ajay was appointed as the in charge for the new case with the dead man in the reservoir that we found today."

"The new case was an exception to the rule, Kevin. This was the last time I had to appoint an in charge person according to the old way of working."

Kevin was looking down towards his feet and thinking deeply. He wanted Alex to know that he didn't believe in Alex's answer. After a little silence, Kevin looked up and stretched his back at the same time. He understood that he couldn't avoid Alex's proposal for very long.

"Now, that I have been thinking about this, I realize that the team model of yours can be a winning solution, Alex. It can also give me the possibility to try new things. Okay, let's give it a try," Kevin finally said.

Alex stood up from his chair with a big smile on his face and he stretched out his hands to Kevin. "I'm glad to hear that you are willing to try, Kevin, and I want you to start right now. I will send out a formal announcement about your new role right away."

Kevin left Alex's office and walked straight to his desk. All the people in the office were looking at him in the hope of figuring out if the meeting was good or bad. This was always the case when anyone exited the boss's office after they were called to meet him.

"I'm alive. I will still work full time. I will be highly productive. I will work together with all of you and be one of the team players; that solves everything," Kevin said with a high voice.

All in the office were smiling as they all understood the sarcasm in the spontaneous speech Kevin gave. He turned his head to the boss's office and he could see Alex looking out to the office floor with a cup of coffee in his hand.

"What happened at the boss's office?" Hamid asked.

"Don't think too deeply on my reaction. Alex offered me a new role in the department. The role is called Senior Advisor," Kevin said.

"What does it mean? What are you going to do as the Senior Advisor?" Hamid asked.

"I don't know. Anyway, I will continue as before, but I'm not going to have total responsibility for myself," Kevin said.

Hamid understood from Kevin's body language and the tone of his answer that he was not happy with his new role. He decided to give Kevin some supporting words.

"You have the longest experience in the criminal investigations area here in the office. You should not be worried about your position. You will not be fired," Hamid said.

"Well, we shall see what comes out of this," Kevin said and looked down into his hands, thinking deeply.

□□□

Kevin walked to the coffee area with the daily newspaper in his hand. Nobody followed him. They all had understood that he wanted to be alone without his colleagues asking questions to him. Ajay arrived in the office in a hurry. He did not greet anybody. He just unpacked his laptop and documents. Kevin saw him arrive, so he walked over to Ajay to see if anything was found in the autopsy.

"Good morning, Ajay I have heard that you have been checking the autopsy result. Any developments?" Kevin asked.

"Yes, there are strange alphabetic characters tattooed on his upper left arm. I have ordered the photographer guy to go there and take some photos of it," Ajay said.

"Alphabetic characters? That is strange. What about the reason for death?" Kevin asked.

"The reason for death is not clear. There are no major marks on the body. They will continue the analysis of samples taken from the body; you know the usual stuff," Ajay said.

"Would be interesting to see the alphabetic characters when the photos arrived," Kevin said.

"Always something to start with. I have also ordered them to take fingerprints," Ajay said.

Hamid was listening to the conversation with interest. He walked to the coffee area and pressed a couple of buttons to get some coffee. Kevin followed him to the coffee room.

"I heard what you talked about with Ajay. Strange right? All the tattooed alphabetic characters are on the upper arm," Hamid said.

"Yes. If you think about it, the characters must be extremely important. Why tattoo them on the upper left arm? There must be an explanation to take such a drastic step of permanently writing the characters on one's body," Kevin said.

Now Ajay also walked into the coffee room and pushed a couple of buttons to get the coffee of his choice. He was looking at Kevin while the machine made whirring sounds.

"Kevin, I heard that you will have a new assignment as a Senior Advisor. Does anybody know who you are going to advise?" Ajay said with a certain smile.

Kevin understood that Ajay intended him to know he did not need any help from anybody. Suddenly Ajay rushed out from the coffee room when he saw the photographer guy arriving with the photos. Ajay got the photos first since he ordered the photos to be taken. Ajay walked slowly to his desk and reviewed the photos focusing on them one by one. Now, Alex also walked to Ajay's desk, to see the photos of the tattoos.

"I saw the photographer guy arriving with the photos. I'm also interested in seeing the photos with the strange characters," Alex said.

Ajay browsed fast through the photo package and picked out three photos for Alex. Alex was looking at the photos carefully.

"Has Kevin seen these photos?" Alex asked.

"No, the photos arrived minutes ago, boss," Ajay said.

"Kevin, have you seen the photos from the body with the strange characters? Come over and look at them," Alex addressed Kevin directly, leaving no room for Ajay to intervene. Kevin walked slowly to Ajay and Alex to look at the photos.

They all stood close together and looked at the photos and changed the photos between them several times.

"Ajay do we have anything else on the case?" Alex asked.

"There is nothing more to work on except these photos. The autopsy shows that he did not die because of drowning. His lungs were not filled with water. The man was already dead before the body was dumped at the reservoir. They will continue the analysis and hopefully, we will get something more," Ajay said.

"Have we sent divers to investigate the bottom of the reservoir where he was found?" Kevin asked. "I noticed that the victim's shoe was missing when he was found at the reservoir" Kevin continued.

"The divers are there right now, so, let's hope they find something," Ajay said.

"Let's take some copies of the photos so we have our own set to work with," Alex said and walked to Amanda with the photo package to be copied. Amanda made the copies and she also studied the photos carefully before returning them.

"Here are the photos. It's really a strange set of characters. I have never seen these types of characters before," Amanda said.

Kevin took his set of photos and walked away to Hamid's desk. Hamid was deeply involved in something that was flashing on one of his displays. Kevin threw the photo package on Hamid's desk to get his attention. Hamid looked up with surprised expressions.

"Here are the photos of the strange characters found on the dead man. I wonder if you can look at the photos and add some value from your area," Kevin said smilingly.

This was the first time that Kevin had asked Hamid about something. Hamid, too, started studying the photos carefully. After a while, he slowly stood up holding one of the photos up in the air. Kevin was watching him surprisingly. Suddenly, Hamid shouted out loudly.

"I know what this means I have seen this before. It's very simple," Hamid said.

Everyone in the office raised their heads and looked at Hamid. Amanda rushed to Hamid to investigate what was going on. Ajay also showed some interest in what was happening but walked slowly to Hamid.

"The characters are tattooed according to the mirror writing concept. This is done by writing in the direction that is the reverse of the natural way for a given language; the result is the mirror image of the tattoo. The characters will appear as normal when they'll be reflected in the mirror. It's a primitive form of cipher writing," Hamid said.

"Amanda do you have a mirror?" Hamid asked.

Amanda nodded and picked up a small handheld mirror from her purse and handed it over to Hamid. He placed the mirror close to the photo so he could read the characters from the mirror. They all turned to reverse across, the way they should be read.

"I can now read the characters correctly. Please write down SCNU," Hamid said.

"Hamid, I'm impressed that you solved this almost directly," Kevin said.

"Well, now we have the characters in the readable order. One thing I don't still understand, what the characters represent," Hamid said.

"I can inform Alex about this cipher that we now have solved. I think this is an important step to solve this case," Ajay said and walked to Alex's office.

The others were looking at each other but no one said anything. They were used to the fact that Ajay always wanted to take the credit for himself, even for things that he had not participated.

After a couple of minutes, Ajay walked out of Alex's office.

"Any comments from Alex?" Kevin asked.

Before Ajay could answer Kevin's question, his mobile phone rang. He was listening intensely what the caller was saying while looking around at the others standing around him. Ajay hung up the mobile after he was done.

"It was the dive manager who called. They have found the other shoe at the bottom of the reservoir. It's now sent for more detailed analysis at the technical investigation department. But that's not all." Ajay said looking around at the others. "Listen all, they have also found a photo in the victim's missing shoe. They will send over the photo right now."

"Wow. That's incredible. We are lucky," Hamid said.

"Well let's wait for the photo to arrive so we can judge if it will bring some new useful information to the investigation," Kevin said.

"Kevin is right. Let's see what we have and decide the next step then," Ajay said.

"I think it's time for lunch. Hamid, can you join me for lunch today? Today I'll pay for the lunch; you deserve it after your achievement," Kevin said.

"Thank you. I appreciate it. You know I usually eat my lunch at home."

"You should have lunch with your colleagues. It's important to know your colleagues and you will get more information about what is going on in the department," Kevin said.

Kevin and Hamid were about to leave for lunch when one of the investigation assistants arrived with the photo found in the dead man's shoe. Kevin and Hamid stayed in the office to join Ajay and Alex to see the photo. There was a Caucasian man in the photo standing alone at an unknown location. The photo had some water damage. They were all now looking at the photo in silence.

"Let's start the search for the unknown man in the photo," Alex said.

"I can recognize the location where the photo was taken. It's close to where I live. The photo is taken at the Bedok Reservoir Park in front of the canoe club," Kevin said.

"Excellent. Now we know the location where the photo was taken, but we also need to find him, the unknown man on the photo," Alex said.

"I think the dead man has some connection to the Bedok Reservoir area. He was found dead there and now we see a photo with an unknown man in the same area," Kevin said.

"Good now we have some investigation to do. I want to have this done with a clear structure and in an organized way," Alex said and started to distribute work tasks to Kevin and Hamid.

"Kevin you should start to talk to people working around the Bedok Reservoir," Alex said. "Hamid! I want you to check how the new technology can be used in this. I guess you have the best knowledge of what is possible here. You work it out exactly what can be done," Alex said.

Ajay was confused and surprised that Alex had taken over the investigation from him. He kept on looking towards Alex but not saying anything.

"Now we all know how to proceed, so let's get going with this and keep me informed," Alex said and walked back to his office.

Ajay was disappointed that he was not asked to direct the others and above all, he did not get any instructions what he should do. Was this move from Alex a sign of mistrust or trust? Ajay was disappointed with this new situation.

Ajay could see that Alex was in his office. Ajay walked to the office and knocked on the door. Alex looked up from the document he was reading. "Ajay what can I do for you?" Alex asked

"I saw that you were in the office, so I saw an opportunity to inform you where we are with the investigation," Ajay said.

"Yes. I must say that the case has high priority at top Management as newspapers and TV channels are reporting the case. We need to communicate soon on what we have," Alex said.

"We need more information about the case before we communicate to the press," Ajay said.

"You are right, Ajay. Let's wait until we have more, and I know you have the capability to bring facts on the table to solve this case. Remember that you are responsible for this case," Alex said.

"Thank you very much. I'm looking forward to doing it," Ajay said with a smile on his face. He was now convinced that Alex had his full trust in him to solve the case. Hamid was sitting at his desk and thinking about Alex's words. "Look at how the new technology can be used." He really did not understand what he should deliver to Alex, so he asked Kevin.

"Kevin, Alex said I can start to look at the new technology and I don't know what he meant?" Hamid asked.

"Do you want to know what I think he means? I think he means that he has no idea what is possible in the technology area and you have free hands. Be happy about that," Kevin said.

"I want to deliver to Alex exactly what he wants, but if he doesn't know what that is then he can't be disappointed at me, can he?" Hamid said, and they were both laughing.

"I have an easy task to talk to the people around the Bedok Reservoir and I can do that easily since it's close to my home. I think I will start with this right now. Meanwhile you, Hamid, need to find a haystack to look into it for the needle," Kevin said and left the office for the day.

□□□

Ajay walked to Hamid's desk with some documents in his hand. Hamid was looking at him with a surprised look as Ajay was standing close to his desk.

"Hamid, I want you to work with the fingerprint results when they arrive. I think they will arrive shortly or tomorrow morning," Ajay said.

"I will take care of that. But I must remind you that I have not done it before," Hamid said and took the document from Ajay.

"Don't worry you will manage, and you can ask the Senior Advisor about it," Ajay said smiling and walked to his desk.

Chapter

2

The next morning the fingerprint analysis report arrived directly to Hamid. He decided to do some investigations for himself before communicating with others. After a couple of hours of his own investigations, he was ready to communicate his findings. So, he entered the coffee room in a hurry to inform Kevin and Ajay.

"I have checked the victim's fingerprints with the border authorities. The dead man has been traveling to Singapore once a quarter. The average length of stay every time was a week. I have checked hotel records and there is nothing. So, he must have stayed somewhere else then. The other information is that he entered Singapore with a South Korean passport. I have checked with the South Korean embassy and they say that he is not a South Korean citizen. They have no records of him, and they clearly said that his passport was a fake," Hamid said and pushed some buttons to select his coffee.

"It seems our hacker is getting things done now," Ajay said laughing.

They took their coffees and sat together at the round table in the coffee room, sipping their coffee and reading some magazines that were lying on the table. Kevin was reading a crime magazine with an interesting article about some new technology that can be used in crime investigations. He wanted to get others' attention to the article.

"Here is an article on a new technology where a computer can recognize a face on a photo. That technology could be useful in our case. What do you say about that Hamid?" Kevin asked Hamid pointing towards the article in the magazine.

"Yes, that technology can be used today. We don't have that technology and there are limited numbers of those available. The equipment is very expensive," Hamid said.

All the investigators left the coffee area and walked to their desks.

"I will take a walk around the Bedok Reservoir and talk to people who were working around that area as Alex requested. See you tomorrow Hamid," Kevin said and walked out of the office.

Hamid was sitting and thinking about the photo recognition program they talked about at the coffee room. Suddenly, he remembered that one of his colleagues in the international technology area can help him. They should know what can be done. He decided to contact his friend Allan McPherson. He was a young man with a stern British accent, working as an IS/IT investigator at Interpol. Allan knew Hamid from several International Crime Investigation Conferences they attended together. They generally contact monthly to discuss different problems in their area. Hamid decided to call Allan for some insights.

Allan picked up and after a few greetings, Hamid informed Allan what he was working on. "Allan, you must help me with this urgent problem. I have a photo of a man and I want you to check him against your new photo recognition system. At one of our international conferences, you told me that you have that system." Hamid said.

"Yes, we do have the right equipment to do that, Hamid! But I will need the approval from my boss before I can help you. Give me a couple of minutes so I can check with him if it's okay," Allan said disappearing from the screen.

Hamid started to play a computer game while he was waiting for a response from Allan. Hamid had three big display screens on his desk. All three were capable of displaying different things at a time. Ajay passed Hamid's desk and stopped a while after noticing that he was playing some sort of computer game. Ajay shook his head in disapproval looking at the screen. Meanwhile, Allan returned to the call and Hamid could see him sitting back on his chair.

"I talked to my boss and he is okay with this support. However, if you find something interesting about this person you must give us all the information. Get it?" Allan said.

"I promise. I will send the scanned photo to you right away." Hamid said. Hamid pressed the send key to transfer the photo to Allan's computer and started to play the computer game again in a high volume this time so it can be heard in the whole office. Amanda walked by Hamid's desk to investigate what was going on. Amanda did not say anything but kept on watching as the game progressed. Kevin was also interested in Hamid's work activities, so he walked to Hamid's desk to look at Hamid's screen. Ajay noted that two more people were now looking at Hamid's display.

"Well, I guess you are all busy with the case, but I can't understand how Hamid's gaming can add value to our investigation," Ajay said.

They all smiled at Ajay's sarcastic comment. He always said something sarcastic when he had the opportunity.

"Yes, we are in full investigation mode right now and I will give you the result of this investigation activity within thirty minutes," Hamid said.

They all smiled at the kids bickering and walked back to their desks. Everything was calm and silent in the office when Amanda was rushing out on the office floor. Hamid stops playing, and Ajay stood up from his chair. Kevin also was looking at Amanda out of his file.

"Listen, everybody. Alex wants to meet all personnel working with the dead man in the Bedok Reservoir case. Let's meet in the conference room right now," Amanda said.

All the investigators walked to the conference room while Alex walked in with a big smile on his face. "I have some good news. We have evidence of creative thinking in this department. Hamid has used a creative idea to bring our case forward by a big step. I'm glad we have some new thinking and well-developed teamwork," Alex said.

Everyone in the conference room was looking at Hamid and his surprised face. Hamid was not clear what this meant; if it was good or bad news for him.

"I have received some good news from the Interpol forensic department. I have some friends there you know since a couple of years ago when I had my training there. Anyhow, Hamid is today's star in the department. He has contacted Interpol and asked for permission to use their new photo recognition technology and he has asked for the info on the photo of the unknown man that was found in the reservoir," Alex said.

Everyone started to smile and nodded at Hamid to his great idea to use Interpol technology in the case. Ajay was looking down to the floor not showing any reaction or appreciation to Hamid. Hamid was smiling and Kevin gave him thumbs up.

"Great work from Hamid and what was the result, do you know? The man in the photo is an internationally recognized Russian arms and weapons dealer. His name is Nikolaj Puchkov. He is wanted in several countries for breaking international trade laws. He is known to sell arms to all the organizations including terrorists that are willing to pay. His major crimes are violations of international embargo treaties and export control regulations in both the US and EU. Any questions?" Alex asked but no questions were asked so he continued. "All this new information was found by Hamid and because of his creative investigation capability. Go out there and find this Russian man and identify the dead man in the Bedok Reservoir," Alex said.

All investigators left the conference room and Kevin walked into the coffee area alone. He could see that all investigators continued with their tasks with high motivation. He was looking deeply into the coffee mug when Ajay entered the room.

"Hi, Kevin! How is your retirement planning going? Have you found any hobbies to start with?" Ajay asked.

Kevin did not answer instead he questioned Ajay. "How is your investigation going now when you have the responsibility?"

"It's going very well. I think we can solve this case very soon," Ajay said with overconfident voice.

They were both standing silently when Amanda entered the coffee room with a serious look on her face.

"Ajay, the boss wanted to see you now. I think it's urgent," Amanda said.

Ajay placed his mug on the table and walked to his desk and picked up a notebook. He was looking at Alex's office and he could see that the curtains were closed. He walked into Alex's office after knocking.

"Hi! Ajay, I wanted to talk to you about the case with the dead man in the reservoir. Where are we and what do we have to work on?" Alex asked.

"Well the dead man in the reservoir entered Singapore with a false South Korean passport and he was identified today. The dead man has a travel record from the border control showing that he has traveled to Singapore on a quarterly basis and stays around one week each time, but we don't know where he stayed. There are no records of the hotels."

Alex took off his glasses slowly and cleaned them with a cloth. He was rocking his chair at the same time. Ajay could see that Alex was unhappy with the progress.

"Well, it's not much. The case is getting more attention and I'm getting more questions about it. How is Kevin engaged in this case?" Alex asked.

"I don't really know what he is focusing on right now. I guess he is planning his retirement," Ajay said with a smile.

Alex stopped rocking his chair and put on his glasses. Ajay understood that his answer to Alex was wrong. Alex stood up and started to walk around in the office.

"You know that Kevin is the best investigator we have ever had and his record of solving cases is excellent. This department is going to be managed with teamwork and that's what I expect from all the people working here including you. I expect more teamwork from you as the responsible for this case. Go out there and improve your team working skills," Alex said.

Alex sat down on his chair and started to read a document without looking at Ajay. This was the signal to Ajay that the meeting was over, and he must leave the office. Ajay walked out from Alex's office in a hurry and walked straight to the coffee room. It was clear to all in the office that his meeting with the boss was not good.

In the evening Kevin was walking along the Bedok Reservoir road to a hawker's place where he ordered BBQ duck, rice and soup set. In the hawker places, you can't order drinks at the same booth as the food. You must order drinks from a specific drinks booth, so he walked there to order his beer. He decided to pull out his photo of the Russian man and showed it to the waitress.

"Have you seen this man before?" Kevin asked the waitress.

The waitress looked at the photo and showed it to another lady behind her. They started to speak in Mandarin in loud voices. Then the waitress turned back to Kevin and answered.

"I don't think I should answer your question, it can be dangerous for me to answer you. I don't know you," the waitress said and gave the photo back to Kevin.

"Sorry that I did not introduce myself. I'm a criminal investigator and here is my badge," Kevin said and shows his badge to the waitress.

"Okay, I understand then I can answer. Yes, I have seen him here together with another person," the waitress said.

"The other person, can you describe him?" Kevin asked.

"He was together with an Asian man. That's the only thing I can remember," the waitress said.

"When was the last time you saw them here?" Kevin asked.

"It's only a couple of days ago. They talked and drank beer together," the waitress said.

"Here is my card and call me at once if you see them here again. I live close to this hawker place so I can be here in five minutes," Kevin said giving the card to the waitress. The waitress looked at the card and nodded in acceptance.

Alex took his beer and walked to his table to eat his dinner. He was sitting and eating alone and thinking about his new role as 'Senior Advisor' and what that meant.

———◆———

PART TWO

Another Dead Body Found

Chapter

3

The next day, two park workers dressed in yellow clothes were cutting the bushes at the Bedok Town Park. They noticed a man sitting on one of the park benches with an umbrella on his lap. It started to rain, and the park workers took cover in their blue truck parked close to the bench. The park workers noticed that the man on the bench did not use his umbrella to cover himself from the rain. They talked about it a while and then they understood that something was wrong with the man. They decided to step out of the truck and check if he was okay. One of the park workers tapped the man on his shoulder but there was no reaction from the man. Instead, the man started slowly to bend forward and finally falling to the ground. The park workers understood at once that the man was dead. One of the park's workers called his manager and inform him that they had found a dead man. The Manager told the park workers to stay where they were and not to touch anything until the police arrived. The Manager called Kevin because he knew Kevin from some other investigations a couple of years ago. Kevin answered his phone seeing an unknown number.

"I understand. Yes. I know where it is. Don't touch anything and close the area from the public until we are there. I will also send an ambulance to the site," Kevin said to the Manager.

Kevin thought a while, and then he walked to Ajay's desk. Hamid was looking at Kevin and trying to understand what the call was all about.

"Ajay, some park workers have found a dead body in Bedok Town Park. I don't know if it's connected to your case. Shall I go there to check this up or do you prefer to take it?" Kevin asked.

"No, you can go and take Hamid with you. I don't think there is any connection to my case," Ajay said.

Kevin nodded and waved to Hamid to follow him. Hamid looked surprised, but he took his headset and walked to Kevin. They informed Amanda where they were going and why, before they walked out of the office area.

"What's happening?" Hamid asked.

"Park workers have found a dead body in Bedok Town Park and we are going there right now. This can be a new case. Anyway, Ajay was not interested so we take it. This will be a good experience for you to see a dead body and arrive as one of the first investigators to a crime scene," Kevin said with a smile.

Hamid was sitting silently in the police car. Kevin could see that he was nervous about the fact that he will be one of the first ones to a crime scene. The police car speeded into the park and the ambulance people were already there. Kevin walked to one of the medical personnel standing beside the ambulance. The medical staff shook their heads to indicate that the man was dead. Kevin walked slowly around the body and around the bench where the man had been sitting. Hamid was standing passively and looking at the dead man lying on the ground with face down.

"Is there anything I can do?" Hamid asked.

"Don't do anything. Don't say anything. What you should do is to just listen to me carefully. I'm going to tell you exactly what I can see here. The best of this is that you are going to write a report on our observations. I guess this will be your first report. Go and get yourself a notebook from the car," Kevin said without looking at Hamid.

Hamid ran to the police car and hurried back. He showed Kevin the pen and the notebook in his hand. The medical person was waiting for the forensic investigators to be ready before they can move the body to be transported. The criminal photographer was taking a lot of photos of the body, park bench, and the surrounding area. Kevin started to describe what he was looking at.

"Hamid, be ready. I will now start to tell you what I see here. The body is lying face down. The man is wearing a short sleeve shirt and black trousers with a black belt. The shoes are brown ordinary walking shoes," Kevin said.

Hamid was now making notes as fast as he could to keep up with the same speed as Kevin was speaking. Kevin waited until he had written down everything that he was saying. "This is a surprise I must say. I can see a tattoo on the man's left upper arm with seven numerals according to the mirror concept. We have seen this before on the man found in Bedok Reservoir. However, this tattoo contains numbers. Get the photographer to come here so we can take some photos of the tattoo."

Hamid waved to a photographer who was standing with the medical personnel. The photographer ran to the scene and took several photos of the tattoo. Kevin could see that the man was shot in the neck at short range. He turned the body slowly so he could take a close look on the dead man's face. When he turned the man, he shook his head slowly.

"Another surprise! I can't believe this. What a coincident?" Kevin said looking at Hamid with a surprised look on his face.

"What do you mean surprise? What shall I note?" Hamid asked.

"This is the Russian man in the photo that was found in the shoe from the dead man in the reservoir. You know the photo where he was standing in front of the kano club at the Bedok Reservoir".

"Are you kidding me? Are you sure, Kevin?" Hamid asked bending down to have a closer look at the man's face. "You are right. This is getting scary. How can this happen?"

The medical team moves the body to the ambulance for the autopsy. The forensic team continued to search the park while Kevin and Hamid drove back to the office. When the forensic team expanded the search area beyond the actual crime place they found a plastic bag under one of the highway overpasses. The plastic bag contained yellow park workers clothes and yellow rubber boots. It was unclear if the content could be connected to the murder of the Russian man, but they decided to send it for analysis anyway.

When Kevin and Hamid arrived at the office and Kevin called for a short meeting with all, to inform them about the findings at the crime scene. Alex decided to join the meeting too.

"Listen to this. Hamid and I have just been to the Bedok Town Park after receiving a call about a dead man there. The interesting thing about this man is that he also has a tattoo. Can you guess where? Yes, on his upper left arm. This man has seven tattooed numbers on the upper left arm. Also, to note that the characters are tattooed according to the mirror concept."

"That's interesting new information and this makes our case even more complicated. Ajay do you have any comments on this new development?" Alex asked.

"No, not really. Who is going to write the crime scene report?" Ajay avoided answering.

"I will write the crime scene investigation report," Hamid said.

Ajay was looking at Hamid with wide eyes full of surprise. Kevin could see that Ajay was surprised that our hacker was going to write the report.

"Don't worry, Ajay. I will guide him in this, and he has been to the crime scene with me," Kevin said.

"I understand and that's okay for me. I guess you do it as a part of your new role as the Senior Advisor," Ajay said with a smile.

All in the room were laughing. They all understood Ajay's sarcastic comment. Kevin and Hamid were also laughing because they did not want to disturb the meeting by starting an argument.

The department phone was ringing, and Amanda walked out of the conference room to answer the call. The others could see Amanda talking on the phone outside the conference room. After a couple of minutes, she entered the conference room with a paper in her hand where she had made some notes.

———◆———

Chapter

4

The next day Amanda rushed into Alex's office and closed the door. Alex was looking up from the document he was reading.

"Good morning Amanda. What's the rush?" Alex asked.

"The Police Commissioner wanted to meet you in her office right away," Amanda said.

The Police Commissioner in Singapore was the highest level in the police force and reporting directly to the Minister of Home Affairs. The position was held by Catherine Zheng. She was a Chinese female of around forty-five years old. She had long black hair and she wore glasses which gave her face a very strict look. Her English was perfect and she had a law degree from the University of London and Singapore. She had also practiced law in a law firm downtown. She was recognized as a brilliant and competent person. Alex was looking at Amanda with a surprised look on his face. He laid down the document he was reading and looked at Amanda for a while before he answered to the request.

"The Commissioner? Why not the Deputy Commissioner, he is closer? I guess the Commissioner has something to say to me directly," Alex said.

Amanda walked out from Alex's office to call for a taxi while Alex collected some documents from the safe at his office. He rode the elevator down to the first floor and the taxi to her office. He arrived at the Commissioner's office and her secretary showed him a place to sit down. After a couple of minutes, the secretary walked to Alex and said in a whispering voice.

"Mr. Alex Hen, you can enter the Commissioner's office now," the secretary said.

Alex knocked on the Commissioner's door and opened it slowly. The Commissioner was sitting with her face towards the window, reading something. Alex marked his presence in the room by a small cough.

They had met before, but she had never called Alex to meet him in her office. Catherine turned her chair to the desk and saw Alex.

"Hi, Alex. Good that you could come on such short notice. Please sit down. The reason I wanted to meet you in person is that we have been approached by one of our allies concerning a Russian weapons dealer that we are investigating. There is high interest from several countries to have this man arrested and to stop his activities. Can you give me a high-level briefing about this case and where we are?" The Commissioner asked.

"Yes, that is right. We have found a Russian person dead on a bench at the Bedok Town Park. We have also found another man floating dead in the Bedok Reservoir. This man is of unknown citizenship, but we are working on it. They are related in some way since both have a strange tattoo on their upper left arm, but we don't know why they had those tattoos," Alex said.

"A tattoo? That is unusual. What type of strange tattoos?" Catherine asked.

"The dead man in the reservoir had four alphabetic characters tattooed on his upper left arm and they were done according to the mirror writing concept. The dead man in the Bedok Town Park did also have a tattoo on the upper left arm with seven numeric characters. The commonality is that they both have the tattoos done according to the mirror concept. The mirror concept is a primitive cipher used to hide what is written in the plain sight, but you can read it when you read it with a mirror," Alex said.

"Interesting and scary at the same time. Now listen carefully. Whatever information we find, in this case, needs to be handled as top secret and only shared with those who have a need to know. Our allies want to be informed about our findings as we move forward with the investigation. Therefore, I request you to report directly our findings to me. I will inform the Minister and he will handle it from there with the foreign office."

"Interpol has also shown interest in this case. They have helped us to identify the Russian man in Bedok Town Park. They also wanted to be informed about this case so how shall we handle their request?" Alex asked.

"Let them know our findings and way forward. Note, however, that I need to know all the facts before they are informed," Catherine said.

"Does this mean that I must come to your office in person to report?" Alex asked.

"No not every time. You can decide the confidentiality level of the information and decide to call or do it in a meeting face to face with me."

"I understand fully," Alex said.

The Commissioner stood up from her chair to indicate that the meeting was over, and Alex left the room.

When Alex returned to his office, he could see Hamid and Kevin sitting in the conference room and he decided to walk into to see how things were going.

"Hi, how are we doing? I see that you are in full speed with the investigation," Alex said.

Before they could answer Alex's question, Ajay walked into the conference room. He had a coffee cup in his hand and seemed to be in a good mood.

"So here are the bright guys trying to solve the mystery of the year. Do we have anything on those numbers and characters?" Ajay asked.

"Well, now when you both are here, we can save time and provide you a short report on what we are working on right now. Hamid, can you take it from here?" Kevin asked.

They had drawn the numeric numbers and the alphabetic characters on the whiteboard. They were trying to figure out what they mean and how they were used.

"The numbers we have are 3,6,0,4,6,2 and 8. These do not represent a phone number. I have checked them to open phone numbers and closed phone numbers from past one year. I have also checked if it represents a Zip code in Singapore or internationally but no hit," Hamid said.

"What about the four SCNU alphabetical characters? Do we have anything on them?" Ajay asked.

"No. Nothing, but we are working on it. Do you have any ideas about it?" Hamid asked.

"No, I have no ideas about it. I just want to inform you that autopsy report is ready. The man in the Bedok Reservoir had a high level of poison in the body. The poison type was used in the Second World War by Russia. The poison stopped the victim's heart within a minute with no other visible damage on the body," Ajay said while sipping his coffee.

"How could the victim get the poison into the body?" Kevin asked.

"Our theory is that it was injected in some way. When the poison was injected the process of death starts at once. This also meant that the killer must be close to the victim. They have to know each other and with this reason, came close to the victim without suspicions," Ajay said.

"Do we know where on the body the poison was injected?" Hamid asked.

"No, we could not find any signs at all on the body," Ajay said.

"Good. Continue with your efforts and see what we can find. If you need help let me know," Alex said and left the conference room together with Ajay.

Ajay could see that Amanda was sitting alone and drinking coffee. Ajay entered the coffee room and pushed the selection of keys to get the right type of coffee.

"I saw that Alex was on the run today. What was that all about?" Ajay asked.

"It was nothing special. He was called to the Commissioner's office and he needed to be there at once," Amanda said.

Ajay was surprised by the answer. He sat down close to Amanda in an attempt to get more information about the meeting.

"Did you say to meet the Deputy Commissioner?" Ajay asked in a surprised voice.

"No. The Police Commissioner, not the Deputy."

"Wow! Do you have any idea what it was about?"

"No, I have no clue what it was about. Why don't you ask him?"

Ajay did not answer Amanda. He walked away with his cup in his hand. Kevin and Hamid were still in the conference room brainstorming to find a solution to the tattooed characters. The investigation seemed to have halted since there was no new information found and the mystic tattoos had no solution. The pressure was increasing on all investigators; especially on Alex with the demand of directly reporting to the Police Commissioner.

———◆———

Chapter

5

The next day, Alex was walking around in the office, looking for somebody to talk to. All the investigators were busy with something. Alex wanted to talk about the dead men with tattoos. But nobody wanted to talk to Alex about it since there is nothing new to talk about.

"Any news on the case? What do we have today?" Alex asked.

"We have nothing new. We are standing still in the investigation," Ajay said.

"This is unacceptable. We can't continue like this. We need to report progress every day. Have you lost your creativity?" Alex said in a high voice that could be heard by all in the office.

They all understand the pressure Alex was under. It was also obvious that Alex was upset about the lack of progress. His voice level revealed his irritation. Alex was standing in the middle of the office floor and speaking in a high voice. Alex kept standing on the office floor for a short while, and then he walked back to his office and closed the door behind him. Amanda walked into Alex's office and talked to him about something and to calm him down. Then Alex again came out of his office and started to talk to everybody, but this time on a lower voice level.

"Listen all, we need to have some good ideas now and we need to be creative on this one. The investigation has been standing still for days without any progress. Where is our hacker; Hamid? He needs to be involved?" Alex said and was looking around in the office.

"I have seen him in the office today, so he should be around here somewhere," Kevin said.

□□□

Hamid's apartment was close to the office. Sometimes he'd decide to take lunch at home. This was one of those days and now he was sitting in his home preparing his lunch in the micro. When he was sitting and eating his mind was thinking about the tattooed characters and what they represented. Then he realized that maybe his friend Allan can help him with this. After lunch he decided to call Allan.

"Hi, Allan. How are you? Any interesting investigations on your side?" Hamid asked.

"Hi, Hamid. Nothing interesting going on; you know the usual stuff. You know it's still early in the morning for me. I guess you are busy with that dead Russian arms dealer and the tattoos," Allan said.

"Yes. We are working full time on that. I must say that our investigation is not going forward. We have no clue about the strange tattooed numbers and characters on the dead men."

"Can I help you with something? I have time today," Allan said.

"Thanks. But I don't have anything specific that you could help me with. I only wanted to talk to you as it's my lunch break right now. I was confused with the numbers and characters we saw on both dead men's arms. They don't make any sense to me. We have checked all the opportunities without any result. Now the upper Management wants new facts every day, but we don't have anything new to report."

"Think outside the box, Hamid. Car registration numbers, postbox numbers, personal bank account numbers, social ID numbers, anything. The numbers are important otherwise they would not have them tattooed," Allan said.

"We understood that the solution must be in those strange numbers and characters. If we solve those then we will bring the case to a solution," Hamid said.

"Yes, you are right; the numbers and characters seem to be the key to solving this case,"

"You know I have to… what... Of course, this is," Hamid said and stopped talking in the middle of the conversation.

Hamid's apartment was on the second floor in an HDB apartment complex so he could see the traffic outside his window. He spotted a truck pulling a shipping container and the shipping container had numbers painted on the side and in the back of it. The same set of numbers as they were working with. Now he could see them together the first time.

"Yes! Of course, it's that. I can see four alphabetic characters followed by seven digits together. This is the solution. Now I know. I got it. Thank you, Allan, for your help. I must go now," Hamid said and disappeared from Alan's screen.

"What are you talking about? What do you mean with seeing characters and numbers? Hello? Hamid, are you there? Can you hear me?" Allan asked but he did not get any answer from Hamid.

Hamid was half running back to the office. When he entered the office, he ran into Ajay and Alex. It looked like they were waiting for him. He stopped right in front of them with a surprised look on his face without saying anything.

"Well, here we have our hacker who will solve the case. I don't think we can solve the case by very long lunches," Ajay said as usual in his sarcastic tone.

"We have been discussing the case and I expected you to be around. You should also tell your colleagues and Amanda where you are going so that we know," Alex said in an irritated voice.

Hamid was so surprised by the comments from Ajay and Alex, so he forgot to tell them about his discovery. He kept standing a short while without saying anything and then he walked slowly to his desk. Kevin was sitting and reading something. He started to talk to Hamid without lifting his head from the document.

"I heard what they said. Don't worry. The pressure is high to find the solution to the tattoos. Now they just let the steam come out on you. It's nothing personal; forget it. I'm thinking about the characters both day and night. What about you?" Kevin asked.

Hamid was now shining up and smiling. He leaned forward closer to Kevin so he could whisper something to him.

"Kevin, I have found the solution. I know what the numbers and characters represent."

Kevin almost fell off his chair and clutched the table to not to. He was leaning back now with a surprised expression on his face. Hamid was looking at him and smiling. Kevin also leaned forward to listen more carefully to what Hamid was saying.

"Are you kidding me or are you serious? We need to talk about this in a closed room. This sounds too much for me."

They walked into the conference room and closed the door behind them.

"Now let's be serious about this. Tell me your story from the beginning so I can believe it."

"I was getting hungry, so I went home for lunch. You know I can walk and be at my apartment in five minutes. At home, I called my friend Allan and to my surprise as he answered, well, I should have known that it was early in the morning for him. We started to talk about daily things when I suddenly spotted a truck pulling a shipping container outside my window. To my surprise, I saw clearly the combinations of characters and digits on the container. Kevin, it's a shipping container number."

"You are a genius. We need to inform the others about this. I want to see Alex and Ajay's jaws dropping when they hear this. You do the talking I will listen and watch their faces and what they propose as actions now," Kevin said.

Hamid was writing down the container number SCNU3604628 on one of the whiteboards. The Characters and digits are written together as they shall appear on the shipping container. Kevin was informing all staff to be present in the conference room to attend Hamid's presentation. Alex and Ajay walked in last into the conference room.

"Well, what do we have here? I hope the bright guys have something worth time spending on since we have other things to do," Ajay said as usual in a sarcastic way and everybody was laughing.

"Welcome all and let's listen to Hamid and what he has to say. Go ahead, Hamid," Alex said.

"The tattoo number SCNU3604628 is a shipping container identification number according to ISO 6346. The ISO 6346 is an international standard used to describe the identification of a shipping container. If you understand what this number means, then you will get a lot of information about the container." Ajay was looking at Hamid with a distasteful expression but Hamid continued. "The first three characters, in our case SCN, show the owner's code. The next character, U, shows the type of the container and in this case with the U, it's a freight container. The following six digits, 360462, represent the serial number and the last digit 8 is the check digit."

Everybody in the conference room was surprised to hear Hamid's solution. They did not have this kind of knowledge about how shipping container identification numbers worked and what they represented.

"Hamid, you are fantastic! Well done. You have just saved this department's reputation. I think that the Harbor Authorities need to know that we are on our way to ask them some questions," Alex said standing up with a big smile on his face.

Spontaneous applause was given by all personnel to Hamid for his excellent result to find the solution to the tattoos. Hamid nodded and lifted his hand to indicate that he was thankful for the recognition of his achievement.

"I will check with the Port Authority, what system they have and if we can get into their system to check the container number. I guess there is an authorization approval to have this access," Hamid said.

"I will inform the Port Authorities that we are on the way and we want to meet some people who can give us answers about a specific container. We need to know if it's in the port or on the way to the port," Ajay said.

The investigators left the conference room in a hurry. Some of them coordinated together who should follow to the Port Authorities and others found their own task depending on the level of experience they had. Kevin was not asked to contribute in any way this time, so he felt a little bit sad about it. Kevin was now sitting alone in the conference room after others have left. Alex noticed that he was alone, so he decided to go back into the conference room and talk to Kevin.

"How are you, Kevin? You seem to be a little down. Anything I can help you with?" Alex asked.

"I was thinking about this meeting. They all had a specific task to do after this meeting, but I did not have anything," Kevin said.

"You are feeling that you aren't contributing. Let me be clear when I say that you are completely wrong. You are coaching Hamid in this and that has already given results. You have a new role now as the Senior Advisor and it's all going well, in fact, better than I expected, Kevin," Alex said looking Kevin straight in his eyes.

Kevin remained silent a while before he commented back on Alex's feedback. "Thank you for those words, I hope this is the reality. You know I'm trying very hard to work into my new role and that is not easy for me. Old dogs you know."

"You shall continue as you have started because we all are making progress both with ourselves and the case we are here to solve. Let's go to work, Kevin."

Kevin nodded and walked slowly out of the conference room without saying anything. Alex kept looking at him when he walked out of the conference room. Most of the investigators had left for the Port Authority. Kevin walked to his desk to figure out his contribution in this case. He was looking at Hamid behind his wall of display screens.

"I hope you are contributing now," Kevin said to Hamid.

"I try hard to contribute but sometimes I don't know if that is the case. Anyhow, today was my day in the conference room to receive applause and it is not an everyday thing," Hamid said smiling.

"I have never gotten any applause in this department. I guess I will get that when I'll announce my retirement day," Kevin said looking out of the office window.

Hamid did not say anything he was looking at Kevin over his wall of displays and shook his head.

———◆———

PART THREE

The Port Authority

Chapter

6

Hamid was typing on his keyboard in full speed and his eyes were moving fast over the display. Kevin was sitting and watching Hamid's keyboard activity.

"I wish I had your competence in finding facts on the computer too," Kevin said.

"Hmm..." Hamid hummed without a straight answer.

"Can I help you with something?" Kevin asked.

Hamid stopped writing and looked over his computer screens. "Sorry, Kevin but I must concentrate on this task, it's important for our investigation," Hamid said and continued his typing on the keyboard.

Hamid was a little irritated by Kevin's questions, so Kevin walked to the coffee area. He returned after a couple of minutes with a cup of coffee in his hand. Kevin could see that Hamid was excited about something when he was reading on the screen.

"Well, what is it? You look so excited. Sorry to ask, but is there something I should know?" Kevin asked.

"Yes. Yes. Yes," Hamid whispered without lifting his eyes from the screen.

"Hamid, please," Kevin said with his hands outreaching like he was waiting for something to drop from the roof.

"Sorry, but now we have it. Now we are in the business with the container number. I have applied for access to the Port Authority's computer systems. I can see the information of all containers on the port; those which are on the way to the port and those which are going to be shipped out from the port."

Kevin walked over to Hamid's desk and leaned over his shoulder to get a firsthand look. Kevin entered the container number SCNU3604628 in the specific field on the display and after a couple of seconds, all the information related to the container number was shown.

"Wow, fantastic. What a technique. It seemed so easy when you did it," Kevin said.

"Here we are, now we can see it. The container is now loaded on a vessel for transport from Rotterdam to Singapore. The vessel is chartered on a monthly schedule between those cities."

"We need to intercept the vessel when it's in Singapore and ask some questions," Kevin said.

"Wait; there is more information like time and date below," Hamid said and continue to read from the display.

The vessel was registered in Rotterdam and it would arrive in Singapore tomorrow morning at five am. The container's content was mentioned as electronics and special steel," Hamid said.

"This is extremely important information and we need to act right away. I will inform Alex and Ajay about this," Kevin said.

Kevin turned and looked at the office, but he could not see Ajay, so he walked into Alex's office. Alex's door was open, but he decided to knock. Alex was looking up from the paper he was reading and showed with his hand that Kevin can come in.

"Alex, we have some good news about the container. We have located it," Kevin said.

"What a progress... that's really good news and you found it so fast. Tell me more," Alex said.

"Follow me and let's go to Hamid," Kevin said.

Alex and Kevin walked to Hamid's desk. Amanda had also joined and now they were all standing behind Hamid's desk looking at the display.

"Well, it seems that our hacker has done it again. You are a fantastic guy, Hamid. You together with Kevin are a team to count on. My theory of teamwork seems to work well," Alex said with a smile.

"I'm glad to have Hamid here. He finds critical information very fast. With the old ways of working, this would have taken much longer time," Kevin said.

"I need to call Ajay and inform him about this. He is on the way to the Port Authority right now to meet the Port Authority Director," Alex said and walked back to his office to call Ajay.

Ajay was sitting in the police car together with several other investigators when his mobile was ringing. He looked at the display and he could see that was Alex calling so he answered.

"Hi, Alex, what can I do for you? Oh really? That's good news. I will inform the Port Authorities about what we already know about the container. Good that we have some time to arrange specific handling of the container when it arrives at the port. Thank you for calling," Ajay said.

The police car with Ajay and his team arrived at the Port Authority and all the investigators were running fast to the reception area. They all drew their police badges before they reached the front desk. The receptionist looked surprisingly at them when they all waved their badges. She did not know that they were criminal investigators since they all were dressed in plain clothes.

"Gentlemen, how can I help you? I can see that you are in a hurry, but you need to sign in any way," the receptionist said.

The investigators were surprised by the demand that they must sign in. Ajay was the first in the queue, so he did the talking for all investigators.

"Here is my police badge and I have an urgent meeting with the Port Director. We have called his secretary to arrange an urgent appointment, so he should know that we are coming," Ajay said.

"You must keep the visitors' badge visible all the time. The Director's office is on the fourth floor," the receptionist said and pointed with the hand to the direction where the elevators were.

The elevator took them up to the fourth floor where the Port Director's secretary welcomed them into a waiting room with a table full of shipping related literature.

"Gentlemen, welcome and please make yourself comfortable. The Director knows that you are here, and he will join you shortly," the secretary said.

The Port Director entered the room in a few minutes. He was a man in the sixties with grey hair and he seemed to be a European. He shook hands with all the investigators and indicated with his hand that they can enter his office and sit down. The Port director's office furniture was made of mahogany and his working desk was big. The whole office was like an old English courtroom.

"Gentlemen, it's not every day that I have visitors from the Crime Investigation Department. I must say I was surprised when my secretary told me that you wanted to have an urgent meeting with me today. What can I do for you gentlemen?" The Director asked.

"We have a case with two men murdered and they were found in different places in the Bedok area," Ajay said.

"Is this related to the case I heard on the news a couple of days ago?" the Port Director asked.

"Yes, that is the case, so let me inform you in more details. We found one dead man in the Bedok Reservoir and the other dead man was found in the Bedok Town Park. The strange thing is that they have characters and numbers tattoos on their upper left arm. One of them had the alphabetic characters and the other had the numbers," Ajay said and pointed with his hand to the upper left arm to indicate the place where the tattoos were located.

"That's unusual and very scary I must say. So, what brought you here?" Director asked.

"The reason we are here is that the combinations of the characters and numbers together represent a shipping container identification number. We have now the information that the actual container is loaded on a vessel that will reach Singapore port tomorrow at five am," Ajay said looking at his watch.

The port director was so stunned by this information. He looked at the other investigators in the room and they were all nodding to confirm what Ajay was saying.

"I'm surprised that you know so many details about the container, where it is and when it will arrive here," the Port Director said.

"Well, it's our job as Criminal Investigators to know the facts," Ajay said, and they all smiled.

"Good to know how much time we have. We must inform the Port Master so we can intercept the container when it arrives to Singapore. Anything else we need to prepare before the container arrives?" the Port Director asked.

"We need to know the handling procedure of the container. Will it remain on or offloaded from the vessel before shipping to another destination? The other critical information we need to know is for how long time the container will be held here in the port?" Ajay asked.

"I understand. Let me talk to my secretary so I can engage the right personnel to help us with this," the Director stood up and walked to the secretary outside his office. The secretary was making a couple of phone calls while the director was standing beside her. After five minutes, the Director and two other people entered the Director's office.

"Gentlemen, these two are from my support team. They will find out all the facts about this container. We have one of the world's most advanced computer systems to keep track of all the containers, vessels entering and exiting the port. Give these men the container number and then we'll know all the facts about the container within a couple of minutes," the Director said.

Ajay handed over an envelope with the container number to the Director. He looked at it shortly and then he passed it on to one of his staff.

"Find out all the facts related to this container. We are going to the coffee area and wait until you have collected all the facts. Call me when you are ready to report your findings," the investigators together with the Director left the room and went to the coffee area.

The Director and the investigators were sitting together talking and laughing when the Director's phone rang and he answered.

"Yes, I understand; we are in the coffee area. Let's meet in my office in about five minutes," the Director said.

"Gentlemen, my staff is now ready to report their findings so let's go to my office," Director said.

All the men walked back to the Director's office. One of the support staff stood in the middle of the room with a document in his hand and he started to read the document.

"Gentlemen the container is loaded and sealed by the Rotterdam customs. The country of origin for the electronics content is the USA and the special steel content is from Germany. The container's destination is China and the customs clearance will be made in the port of Shanghai. This way of handling it is called transshipment. Transshipment will take place in Singapore with the container on hold in the port for twenty-four hours before loading on a Chinese vessel and transported to the port of Shanghai. The container is owned by a container leasing company in South Korea and they are operating hundreds of containers in their fleet, so there is nothing strange with that. Both vessels have valid licenses to enter the port of Singapore."

"These containers will not be opened in Singapore. Is that correct?" Ajay asked.

"That is correct, Sir. They will not be opened here and only to be loaded on the other vessel to China," one of the staff answered.

"What about the company in China who is the formal receiver of the container? Do we know anything about that?" Ajay asked.

"Yes, the receiving company, the one responsible for the customs clearance, is a registered company in Shanghai and they have had container shipments through Singapore for several years. The container will be offloaded from the vessel at five am tomorrow. We have more detailed information about this if needed," the staffs person said.

"Thanks, I think we got all we need for now. What is the next step in this now?" the Port Director asked.

"We need all the access permits to the port so that we can intercept the container and open it. Time is short and we have only twelve hours to work with. Can you arrange all the valid badges and inform the Port Master about our intentions? We need to be aware of the container's location all the time when it's in the port," Ajay said.

"The Port Master will meet you at the gate when you'll arrive. He will also show you the location in the port where we plan to offload the container. Contact the main gate at the port when you arrive, and we will have everything ready for you. I will also inform the Customs about this so they can be there to cut off the Rotterdam seal from the container," the Port Director said.

"We will be there before five am tomorrow. I want to see with my own eyes when the container is offloaded from the vessel," Ajay said and stood up to indicate that the meeting was over.

They have now had received all the necessary pieces of information they needed to proceed. They all shook hands and then left the Port Director's office, escorted by his secretary to the elevators area. The investigators returned their visitors' badges and left the building. Ajay decided to call Kevin from the car.

Kevin was home eating some leftovers from yesterday. The phone rang and he picked it up to check who was calling. When he saw it was Ajay calling he answered.

"Hi, Ajay. What's on your mind at this late hour? I'm not used to getting your calls so late," Kevin said.

"I know it's late and I'm sorry to disturb you but it's urgent. I need men from our department to be at the port tomorrow morning before at five am. We are going to intercept the container and open it for inspection. The offloading will start at five am tomorrow. I want you and Hamid to be there also. Is it possible for you to be there? And can you check with Hamid if he can participate?" Ajay said.

"Yes, of course, I will be there, but I cannot promise that Hamid will be there too. I will call him and confirm."

"Great. Send a message to me when you have Hamid's answer. I think this will increase his competence to be in a port environment in the morning hours," Ajay said laughing.

Kevin finished his dinner before he called Hamid. Hamid was in his apartment playing a computer game. Hamid was using his headset that gave him free hands to play the computer game at the same time as he spoke on the phone.

"Kevin, I'm surprised that you are calling. I'm honored to receive your call at this late hour," Hamid said.

"That was funny. I have a mission for you tomorrow at five am. You need to be at the port to intercept the container. The police units and Customs are going to be there also, so we will not be alone. I hope you can be there, Hamid," Kevin said.

"It's a very short notice I must say. I guess I need to wake up around four am to make it in time," Hamid said.

"I will call you and wake you up. I will pick you up at half past four am tomorrow. This is a great opportunity for you to see some action."

"Your service to wake me up and to pick me up is most welcomed. Okay, I will go there."

"Great, I will send a message to Ajay to inform him that you will arrive with me to the port."

The next morning Kevin picked up Hamid as promised, and they reached the port in time. It was still dark outside and when they watched from a distance when the container was lifted off the vessel.

"I can now see the container's number clearly. This is the container that we were waiting for," Kevin said and gave the binoculars to Hamid.

Hamid was looking at the container in silence. Two Customs officers were standing beside him. The container was loaded on a truck and transported to a specific location at the port. This was done so that the investigators and Customs can work with highest possible discretion. Kevin and Hamid were following the container closely from the Port Master's car. When the container was placed on the ground and the pulling truck had left the area. All involved people took a couple of steps back from the container door when the Customs officials were cutting off the customs seal. They open both doors slowly. The first person to enter the container was Ajay and he had a flashlight in his hand to see in the darkness inside the container. All others stood outside waiting for Ajay's signal.

"Well, it's not completely filled with any equipment; the container is more or less half full. Here are some special steel rolls and several big closed wooden boxes. We need some tools to open the boxes," Ajay said.

Ajay tried to move one of the wooden boxes with his hands but had no success.

"We need a forklift also to lift the boxes out of the container. They are heavy," Ajay said in the darkness.

"I can take care of that," the Port Master said and started talking into his handheld radio to request tools and a forklift. After a couple of minutes, a forklift arrived with a box of tools loaded in it. At the same time, the criminal photographer arrived too. Ajay stood in the middle of a spontaneously formed ring of men dedicated to this mission.

"Listen, all. We are now fully staffed to start the formal inspection of the container content. Let's do it in a systematic way. Our Customs officials have requested to put numbers on each item and describe what it is. We have to do this together and the investigators' name will be written down who picked it out from the box," Ajay said.

All the wooden boxes were now placed out in a row outside the container. Customs officials were writing down all the facts from every box and photos were taking of every box. The first wooden box was opened by a Customs officer and that box contained electronic components of different types and technology levels. There were also some small boxes inside the bigger wooden box that contained advanced chips. Other boxes contained equipment that looked like ordinary water pumps and valves. There were a total of sixteen wooden boxes. The content didn't make any sense, and nobody knew what it was or what it was used for.

"Kevin, what do you think about this?" Ajay asked holding a little chip in his hand.

"I don't want to guess but the content must be extremely important. I think that we need help from the technical department to look at this. Hamid, can you call them after all it's your old home organization," Kevin said holding a piece of a strange form of a pump in his hand and holding it against the morning sun that had started to shine.

Hamid called his former boss and told him about the situation and the urgent assistance they needed. He promised to send a senior person right away to check the container content. After twenty minutes the technical investigator arrived with his special equipment. He started to check the smaller electronic components with the equipment he had with him. Kevin and Hamid were watching him when he was picking up components from the wooden boxes. They noticed that he was shaking his head every time he checked a component.

"I hope he has the right competence to do this work," Kevin said to Hamid.

"Based on the complicated equipment that he has with him, it seems that he is the right man," Hamid said.

The investigator from the technical department walked to Kevin and Hamid with one of the components in his hand.

"I can't say what this is or what it's used for. It's a puzzle of electronic parts and the level of technology is so different," the technical investigator said.

"What is your best guess?" Hamid asked.

"Well, I'm not authorized to guess. My guess can be used as the found facts. That's why I never guess. When I don't know, I say 'I don't know' and there can never be any misunderstanding," the technician said with little irritation in his voice.

Ajay had also joined the discussion with the technician.

"We understand what you are saying. However, we will refer to your words that you could not decide what the content is and what it can be used for. Is that okay for you?" Ajay asked.

"That's okay for me. I'm sorry that I could not help you with this," the technician said and started to pack his instruments.

"This is also difficult for us to write down in our report. We write down each piece individually and not what you can build off them," the Customs official said.

"What is your opinion of this? I guess you have seen a lot of container openings here at the port?" Ajay asked the Port Master.

"That is correct I have seen a lot down here, everything from dead bodies, dead animals to most strange equipment. For most of our cases, we trust the Customs declarations to understand what's inside the containers. I can't say what we are looking at here," the Port Master said.

The technical investigator, Ajay, Kevin, and Hamid were standing in a circle and discussing what was to be done. They had never been exposed to this kind of decision or technology.

"We need to hold the container in the port for further investigations. We can't take this decision. It must be taken higher up in the Police Force," Kevin said.

"Kevin is right; we should call Alex," Ajay said.

Ajay called Alex to inform him about the findings and what the situation was. Alex was upset when he received Ajay's report. Alex was walking around in his office while talking loudly to Ajay.

"Did I hear you correctly that you don't know what the container content is? Are you serious about this? You have several men out there and you can't understand what you are looking at. So, you need a decision to hold the container in the port until we know what the content is. To hold a vessel in the port can be costly and could also have a business impact for the whole Port. I need to contact the Commissioner about this," Alex said.

"We'll stay here until you call back and guide us what to do now," Ajay said.

"It can take time to reach her, so you better eat," Alex said and walked in a hurry to Amanda to arrange the meeting with the Commissioner.

Kevin and Hamid were standing close to Ajay so they could listen to the conversation with Alex. They both nodded to support Ajay in the decision. The technical investigator stayed to watch over the container when Kevin, Hamid and the Port Master left the area for lunch.

———◆———

Chapter

7

The Commissioner could meet Alex in an hour. It was unusual to get a time slot with the Commissioner the same day the request for a meeting is made. Alex took a taxi downtown to meet the Commissioner. The secretary took him into the Commissioner's office directly.

"Welcome, Alex, and sit down, please. I'm really interested in your findings. What do you have?" Catherine asked.

"When we combined the tattoos from the two dead men, we found out that the characters were representing a shipping container registration number. The actual container had arrived at five am this morning and it was offloaded from the vessel," Ajay said.

"That is an unusual development, I must say. I have never heard about this type of connection between the two victims. Please continue."

"The vessel is registered in Rotterdam. The next planned route for the container is China and customs clearance was to be made in Shanghai. The container content owner was a registered company in Shanghai. The content was declared in Rotterdam as special steel and electronic components," Alex said.

"I guess you have opened the container for inspection? You have the authority to do that," Catherine said.

"Yes, we have opened the container and tried to analyze the content together with the technical department and the Customs. The problem is that we don't understand what the content is."

"Hmm... then it's a very special case where special competence is required. From which countries are the contents coming from?"

"The Country of Origin is defined as; for electronics, USA and special steel from Germany. The electronic parts are on different technical levels; everything single components to advanced memory chips."

"You know that we have an agreement with our allies to inform them when we know the container content. I think we need international help to understand the content. You can request Interpol for assistance in this case."

"We have only about twenty hours to decide what to do before the container is loaded on the vessel with onward destination China. I need a decision to hold the container in the port until we understand the content," Alex said.

"I need to call for an urgent meeting with the whole Police Commissioner Committee today. This is complicated and has consequences for the Singapore Port and our relations with other countries," the Commissioner said.

□□□

The Police Commissioner's secretary started to call all the Committee members to the urgent meeting. There were several members of the Government as representatives at the Committee meeting.

The chairman for the Commissioner Committee meeting was Mr. John Lok reporting directly to the Minister of Home Affairs. He was around sixty-five years old with gray hair and was always well dressed in a perfect suit. He had a background as an Attorney and from criminal departments. The members were now gathered in the conference room. The members were a little bit upset about the short notice; however, most of them were in town, so their travel time was relatively short. They were used to have a couple of days to plan their participation but that was not the case this time.

"Welcome to this urgent meeting on such short notice. We have an important decision we need to take today. The time is two pm. The Commissioner will present the case," the chairman said.

The commissioner presented the facts in the case with two men murdered, tattoos on their arms, and container with the unknown content now at the port with a critical timeframe for the decision before it will leave for China. The Foreign Affairs representative argued that the container needed to be held in the port for further investigations to understand the content.

"We have trade regulations that we are committed to enforcing." The Trade & Industry representative argued to release the container according to the actual time plan. This was to avoid implications in trade relations and the potential damage on the port's international reputation.

The Finance representative argued to let the container leave according to the time plan. He did not give any explanation about why he preferred this decision.

The Defense representative said, "It should stay in the port until the content is fully known and understood. We should not let anything pass our ports if we don't know what it is."

The Security representative agreed with the Defense. "Yes, I agree we should hold the container in the port until we know what the content is and how the content can be used."

"Finally, what is the Police Commissioner's opinion in this case?" the Chairman asked.

"We should hold the container in port until we understand the content and how the material can be used. The reason for this is that the container is now an important part of an ongoing murder investigation. This explanation should be acceptable by all involved parties without creating disturbances in our port business or relations with other countries," Catherine said.

Some of the members nodded and some of the members did not express any support to Catherine's view. The Chairman was now ready to make a summary of the members' views.

"I have noted that there is no need for me to use my overall ruling vote in this case. I want to thank Catherine's brilliant argument because of why this decision was taken. For the record, we shall note that this meeting has decided to hold the container in the port for further investigation. The action is now for the Police Commissioner to communicate this decision to those who need to know. The meeting is now formally closed," the Chairman said, and all members left the conference room.

Catherine hurried out from the conference room to call Alex about the decision. Alex had been waiting for the call, so he answered immediately.

"Hi, Catherine. Yes, I understand, it's the right decision. I will call my men at the port right away. They are at the port waiting for the decision right now." Alex called Ajay at the port right away to give him the no loading decision.

"Hi, Alex. Okay, no loading. I will communicate the decision right away," Ajay said.

"Listen, all. We have a no loading decision by the Committee. The investigation can continue until further notice. The directive is also that we have to transport the container out from the port to a more secure location," Ajay said.

The Port Master gave the order for no loading. The Chinese vessel Captain was informed that the vessel must leave the port without the specific container. Kevin and Hamid were overseeing the repacking of the container and the Port Master had arranged a truck to transport the container outside the port to a hangar for further investigation. Kevin and Hamid were standing and watching when the truck was rolling out from the port followed by a single police car with flashing blue lights.

"Well, I think we are going to spend some days at the hangar to check the content," Kevin said as they all sat down in the car to follow the transport to the new location.

The hangar was a huge old Air Force hangar with open floor space to lay down all material that was going to be investigated. When the investigators arrived at the hangar, they started to unpack the container together with the Customs personnel to secure the numbering of all pieces correctly. When the container was emptied, and all the material was lying on the hangar floor it was time to leave for the day. Special Police Force was ordered to guard the hangar under the night. Alex had called in all the investigators to a morning meeting at the office. All personnel were now sitting in the conference room. Alex was standing in front with a piece of paper in his hand.

"Welcome. We now have a decision that gives us almost unlimited time to solve the container content mystery. How long it will take... we don't know. I think that we only need to find a single part in the content that will open our eyes to understand what we are looking at. This is a very special investigation and we have never done this before. We need high technical competence to work with this investigation," Alex said, and everybody nodded.

"The decision also gives us the possibility to request support from other criminal investigative organizations. I have, therefore, requested expertise from Interpol to help us. They will provide two men and those men are right now on the way to join us. I have also appointed Kevin and Hamid to work closely with those men to understand the container content. Ajay will continue to be responsible for the murder investigation of those two men. Questions?" Alex asked.

There were no questions about the new development of taking external help and to split the whole investigation responsibility into two parts. Everybody was looking at Ajay to see his reaction now when Kevin and Hamid have the container investigation responsibility. Ajay did not show any reaction at all.

"Amanda, you have some work to take care of the external personnel when they arrive," Alex said.

"I will provide the Interpol guys with all the badges and access to the premises. I guess they don't need any specific office desk. They are going to be working outside the office most of the time," Amanda said.

All personnel left the conference room. Ajay stopped Alex and requested to have a meeting with him. They both walked into Alex's office and closed the door behind them.

"What can I do for you, Ajay?" Alex asked.

"I was surprised that you let Kevin and Hamid take care of the container content investigation and my role is now reduced to focus on the murder of the two men. I think we should keep the case together and both parts should be handled by me as responsible," Ajay said.

"I understand your reaction, but this is now two separate cases. The container content case has an impact on our national security, trading reputation and implications in relation with other countries. Special reporting to the Commissioner is also required," Alex said.

Ajay didn't say anything, but just stood and listened to Alex's arguments. Alex took a pause and continued. "We have also the Interpol involvement to support us and they will also report to their organization what we are doing. This is a completely new situation that we are not used to handle," Alex said.

"I understand the complications in this case, but I think I can handle both views in this case. I'm starting to think that you don't trust my capability," Ajay said.

"This is not about trust or mistrust. This is to use the personnel resources we have the best possible way. I have full trust in your capabilities, that is not the reason for this change, so don't even think about it. Go out there and find the solution to the two murdered men," Alex said with irritation in his voice.

Alex's answer was straight forward and without any reservations. Ajay realized that there was no point to discuss this matter further. Ajay left the office and walked straight to the coffee area. Amanda was there sitting alone reading some documents.

"I could see that Alex was walking around in his office when he talked to you. He always walks around when he is upset with something," Amanda said.

"No, not really. I asked him some questions and then he was irritated about it," Ajay said.

"Kevin and Hamid are now responsible to investigate the container content. I guess you understand that they have their own case. You sound unhappy with that?" Amanda asked.

"Not really, I know that this case has become too complicated to keep together as one case and managed by one person. I know that the pressure to solve the case is high now on Alex. Did you know that Alex must report directly to the Commissioner on a regular basis about this case?" Ajay asked.

Amanda was listening but did not comment further. She had high integrity to keep all reporting structures strictly to those who need to know.

❑❑❑

The next day in the morning Kevin and Hamid arrived at the hangar with higher self-confidence than before; after all, they were now responsible to solve the container content. The Interpol personnel arrived at the hanger at the same time as Kevin and Hamid. They informed the Interpol persons about the case and the overall objective to understand the use of the material lying at the hangar floor. Somehow, they were already well informed about the case. The Interpol investigators started at once to do their investigation systematically. They wanted to have specific parts placed on a table where they could be examined more deeply with the special instruments that they had brought with them. Other parts that did not need any special inspection were kept back on the floor. Several of the boxes contained advance circuit boards with memory chips. One of the Interpol investigators was looking into one of the memory boards with special equipment. He started to talk at the same time as he was looking into a flashing screen with several numbers passing. Kevin and Hamid stopped beside his table to listen to what he had to say.

"I'm looking at something that you need to know. This memory board is storing coordinates and other geographical data. This equipment is used for navigation and it has the world map stored with the reference points," the Interpol investigator said.

Kevin and Hamid looked at the display without saying anything, they continue to the next table. The other investigator from Interpol was looking at some special valves made of special steel. He was turning the valve around in his hand and measuring the channels in the valves and making notes at the same time. Kevin asked him about his theory of the parts.

"What do you think of that valve in your hand?" Kevin asked.

"I think this valve is used in a very specialized application. The valve I'm looking at here is not for ordinary applications like cars or other daily machinery. It has a much more specialized application due to its extremely small size and type of material it's built from," the Interpol investigator said.

Metallurgical analysis of the steel roll metal has been performed in Germany. The result has arrived filled with interesting facts about the use of this steel. Kevin had called all people working at the hangar to discuss the findings. They were all now sitting together in a small room at the hangar.

"Welcome. We have some interesting findings and conclusions. We have a navigation gyro with navigation maps stored in memory chips. We have valves specialized for very small application and not used in ordinary machinery. We have special steel that is used mainly in hot applications to resist high-temperature changes with fast variation in the heating cycle. Let's discuss what we think is lying here," Kevin said.

"I think its parts to build a steel iron mill of smaller size. Valves are for gas to the heating and steel for the process that can resist high temperatures," one investigator said.

"I think they are parts for a nuclear submarine based on the valves I have examined and the steel for the reactor area in the submarine," one of the Interpol investigators said.

"Both of those theories were close but missing the explanation of how the gyro circuit board with world map reference points fit into those scenarios. All reference points on the memory board are on land and not in the sea," Hamid said.

"I agree with Hamid. The gyro board for navigation is the key to this puzzle. Steel mills are not moving around. Let's continue our search to find a common proposal what the parts can be used for," Kevin said.

The investigators were now discussing in smaller groups to find the solution. Some were going outside the small office and making drawings on the concrete hangar floor to explain their views. Suddenly one of the members in a small group were shouting and waving their hands in the air. All other groups surrounded them to listen to what solution they had found. Hamid was one of the members of the team and he started to explain.

"Our group's understanding is that we are looking at spare parts to build an intercontinental missile. Everything points in that direction. The gyro board is for navigation, small valves to regulate missile fuel and special steel to resist the heat from the exhaust when the missile is in flight. This is our common understanding," Hamid said.

All participants agreed with the theory presented by Hamid. It must be that application this material is used for. Now, the work had begun to find material that deviated from the agreed theory.

"All parts on the hangar floor need to match our theory. Parts that we found that don't match our theory are placed in a specific area. We are getting closer to find a solution, so let's keep a high focus on this," Kevin said.

All investigators were working intensely on the hangar floor. Kevin and Hamid were walking together around the parts and discussing if the agreed theory had any weak links.

"Should we report our findings? What do you think?" Hamid asked.

"Remember that we only have an agreed theory that we can inform Alex about. We must eliminate all the weak links and put all found parts into our theory to see if they can be used to build the missile. I will call Alex and inform him what our main theory is," Kevin took out his phone to call Alex.

"Kevin, you have good news, I hope?" Alex asked.

"Possibly, yes. I have only a short report of our theory right now. Remember it's not verified totally but we are working on it. We think in our theory that the material can be used to build an intercontinental missile with the capability to load a nuclear warhead."

Alex was surprised and silent on the phone for almost a minute. Kevin waited for his comment. Finally, he started speaking. "I could never think of this type of use. It's a surprise. This will have international implications and impact on everything we do from now. You are now focused to eliminate all weak links I hope?" Alex asked.

"Yes, of course, that's what we are doing right now. We have not found anything in the container yet that will crash our theory," Kevin said. "This is highly classified military technology. This technology is so advanced that we need help from an independent third-party organization that can verify our theory."

"I will take care of that," Alex said and hung up the phone before Kevin could ask about what kind of third party support he will use to verify the missile theory.

"What did Alex say about our theory?" Hamid asked.

"Well, he was surprised. He wants to use a third party competence to verify our theory. I don't know who he will send and when they will show up. It'll be interesting though," Kevin said.

Now they saw that Ajay had arrived at the hangar and he was walking around and talking to the Interpol people. He seemed interested to know what the latest findings were. Hamid could see Kevin's face and the expressions that he didn't like Ajay digging around in his area. Kevin and Hamid decided to approach him.

"I see that you are interested in our activities," Kevin said.

"I'm trying to understand more about the murdered men and the connection to the container content. What is your theory about the content?" Ajay asked.

"We have several theories, but we need to analyze all parts to secure that they match one theory. We will probably find parts that don't match our theory also," Kevin said.

"I understand. Ordinary criminal investigation thinking I must say," Ajay said.

Kevin did not answer Ajay. Ajay understood the message that he should not ask more about Kevin's responsibility area. Ajay left the hangar slowly while Kevin kept looking at him when he left.

Suddenly two men in dark suits entered the hangar and they started to walk around and looking at the parts specifically the electronics lying on one of the tables in the hangar.

"Do you know those men, Kevin?" Hamid asked.

"I guess those are the third party guys that Alex was talking about. They have passed the security check, so they are authorized to be in here. They must be Alex's men but let's go and check if that is the case," Kevin said.

Kevin and Hamid walked to the two men in black suits and introduced themselves to the men and they shook hands. They presented themselves with names only and nothing more... no country, no organization or technical department. Since they didn't want to reveal more about their background Kevin did not bother to ask. They were carrying highly classified badges around their neck, so they were authorized to be there.

"We have been requested to support you to verify your theory about what these parts can be used for and what can technically be built with them. Alex has authorized us, and he provided all necessary clearance to visit this premise," one of the agents said.

"So, you are friends to Alex, I guess?" Kevin asked.

"Yes. Alex has worked together with us at our department overseas," the other agent said.

"I understand and welcome to help us. Feel free to ask questions and walk around as you wish. This is my colleague Hamid," Kevin said.

The agents shook hands with Hamid and started walking around in the hangar. Kevin and Hamid were looking at them when they walked around the hangar.

"Alex has a lot of friends overseas. You never know who will show up when Alex requests for help from overseas organizations," Hamid said.

The men in black preferred to work alone. All the electronic components were analyzed with advanced technical instruments. The valves dimensions were measured. The steel rolls metallurgic structure report was read carefully. All findings were supporting the theory that the container content material can be used to build an intercontinental missile.

The next day Alex called all investigating personnel, the Interpol men, and the Men in Black to the Criminal Investigation Department office.

"Welcome to this meeting. The purpose of this meeting is to have an agreement and to verify that our theory is correct; that we are looking at an intercontinental missile's spare parts. I will let one of our overseas colleges explain the findings," Alex said and one of the men in black stood up and started to explain.

"Thank you, Alex. The overall findings indicate that it's possible to build three intercontinental missiles with the parts. Some of the parts are spare parts to the three missiles. It's also possible to add nuclear warheads in those missiles. However, there are more indications to our conclusion. Some of the parts can be used in nuclear production plants. This is a strong indication that somebody has the intention to produce nuclear material and load it as warheads on the missiles. This is serious if it ends up in the wrong hands," the agent said and sat down. Alex stood up to talk.

"We have now the final analysis result so let's close this part of the investigation. We need to pack the container content exactly as it was when we opened it. We have all the documentation and pictures about how it was packed. Kevin and Hamid will coordinate this. I also want to thank everybody for the support you have provided to find the answer to this. I will inform the Commissioner of our findings and I guess we need some directions for the next

step. Any questions about this conclusion or way forward?"
Alex asked.

There were no more questions and they all felt satisfied by their findings. The Interpol men and men in black stood up to thank the investigators for their cooperation. All investigators left the conference room. The agents and the Interpol people stayed in the conference room together with Alex. He wanted to thank them for the support and for the work well done. The Interpol men gathered their equipment and gave all their notes to Amanda for safe storage. The men left the office to the airport and flight home. Kevin could see how relieved Alex was now when he could report that the container mystery was solved. Kevin took the opportunity to talk to Alex outside the conference room.

"I must say, those men were professional with their work. Very systematically they checked all the parts and components. I guess you know those men from before?" Kevin asked.

"Yes. I know them very well. I have worked with them overseas a couple of years ago in my international training," Alex said.

"Yes, they did say that. We did not have that opportunity to work abroad and establish contacts with other criminal investigation organizations in the old days," Kevin said. "That's the good side of this profession; the possibility to work abroad with colleagues."

Kevin walked to Ajay's desk with a smile on his face and a cup of coffee in his hand.

"Now you know that we have the knowledge what the material in the container is used for. I guess my part of the investigation is finally done. Where are you in the two dead men investigation?" Kevin said and sipping his coffee.

Ajay waited a while before he answered. It looked like he needed time to find the correct answer.

"Your container content analysis is valuable information for my part of the investigation. Now we know that the men were killed because of the valuable content in the container. Somebody wanted to take the content and those men were in the way and had to be eliminated," Ajay said.

Kevin was standing and smiling like a big winner and Ajay knew that Kevin's intent was to make him feel like a loser. Both men knew that there was no point to continue the discussion. Kevin walked back to his desk and Ajay started to read a document.

Alex was in his office planning for reporting to the Police Commissioner. This time he knew he can present some progress in the case and he was pleased with his department's performance. He took a taxi to the commissioner's office as usual. He walked into the Police Commissioners office in time. Before Alex sat down on the sofa in the waiting room, the Commissioner's office door opened and she walked into the waiting room.

"Welcome, Alex. It seems that you are a frequent visitor to my office nowadays. I heard you are ready with the container content analysis and now you want to report to me," Catherine said

"With the Interpol's help as you approved and help from my international counterparts, we think we have the full understanding what the container content is. The overall summary is that, with the parts in the container, it's possible to build three intercontinental missiles. There are also some spare parts to those missiles. Those missiles can be loaded with nuclear warheads. The container also held parts used in nuclear production plants and that indicates the intention to produce the nuclear material and load it as a warhead on those missiles. This is serious material if it ends up in the wrong hands," Alex said.

Catherine was silently looking at Alex for a long time. She was surprised about the content and how it can be used.

"Now, I understand. This was not what I expected but now it all makes sense and the puzzle is solved," Catherine said.

"Sorry, Catherine, but what makes sense and what puzzle?" Alex asked.

"We have received information that a North Korean vessel has been meeting our Chinese ship in the middle of the South China Sea. You know the Chinese vessel that was chartered to transport the container to China. Now we suspect that this container was planned to be delivered to North Korea and picked up by the North Korean vessel in the South China Sea. I guess the North Korean vessel Captain was disappointed when he was informed that there was no container to deliver to his vessel," Catherine said.

"Is this illegal to do or what is the problem?" Alex asked.

"There is an international embargo in force against North Korea. To trade with North Korea and especially with highly sophisticated electronics used for intercontinental missiles. Also, to export material that can be used for nuclear production is an international crime. There is severe consequences for companies that violate the international embargo," Catherine said.

"Now I understand the high value of the container content. In fact, so valuable that people can be murdered to get their hands on it. What shall we do know? I need directions on how to proceed," Alex said.

Catherine turned her chair against the office window and started looking out and thinking deeply. She was looking at all the international vessels anchored outside her window. They both now understood that the next decision was not going to be Police organization people's decision. The case has now evolved into a complex international and national security matter. Catherine started to analyze the situation.

"Alex, some facts first. We have the container content in our possession. The material never reached North Korea from Singapore and that is good, and we will be recognized for this. The next question is who owns the container content; the suppliers in USA and Germany or are they now ours. Shall the material be used for further investigation in Rotterdam, where the container was loaded or the USA, where the most critical electronics were coming from? This has now become even more internationally complicated," Catherine said.

"What is your view on this and what is next step we should take?" Alex asked.

"It's Friday afternoon. I will call a meeting with the Police Commissioner's Committee first thing on Monday morning. I will call you about the next step when we have the Commissioner's Committee decision. Have a nice weekend Alex," Catherine said and turned the chair against the window and Alex knew that he should leave the office.

"Have a nice weekend," Alex said and walked out of the office.

Catherine was looking out from the office window and thinking about the complexity of this case and what was the right way forward. There were several international laws that can be applicable in this case and to consider what was best for the nation. She asked her secretary to call an urgent Commissioner's Committee meeting on Monday morning.

☐☐☐

Alex arrived back at the Criminal Investigations office. He could see Amanda standing in the middle of the office floor surrounded by Ajay, Kevin and Hamid.

"Do we have a problem… a new case or what?" Alex asked.

"No, not at all. We are just discussing what happens now that we know the content. Have you received any guidelines from the Commissioner?" Amanda asked.

"The decision will be taken by the Police Commissioner Committee on Monday," Alex said.

"I guess, Hamid and I have done our part of this case for now," Kevin said.

"Yes, for now. You should go home for the weekend and rest. You have done fine so far with your mission." Alex said and walked into his office.

Kevin and Hamid left the office for the weekend, but Ajay was still sitting on his desk and working with something. He was always the last person to leave the office on Fridays. Amanda was also packing her things for the weekend and passed Ajay's desk, so she decided to talk to him.

"Ajay, you are always the last one to leave the office on Fridays. Is there any specific reason for that?" Amanda asked.

"No, not really. I like to work when it's quiet and everybody has left the office," Ajay said.

"I know that you have a wife and children. I think you should be with them on Fridays when you can," Amanda said.

"Amanda, thank you. I'm fine. Have a nice weekend," Ajay said to indicate that he did not want to talk about that topic anymore.

"Have a nice weekend," Amanda said in a worried tone. Amanda left the office and Ajay continued to write on his laptop.

———◆———

PART FOUR

The Transport

Chapter

8

It was the Monday morning and the Commissioners Committee had gathered in the conference room. The last person to walk into the meeting was Catherine and she always walked in together with the Commissioner's Chairman.

The Commissioner's Chairman stood up and opened the meeting. "Welcome to this meeting. I can see that all members of this Committee are here today. We shall decide today on a complicated and important matter. Catherine can start as usual to present the facts on this case."

Catherine started to present the results from the container content analysis. The Committee members were shocked and surprised. They were also pleased by the fact that the shipment did not reach North Korea. The Foreign Affairs argued that the container should be sent back to Rotterdam and the concerned countries can continue their investigation from there. The Defense said that it should be sent back to the countries where the equipment's last Customs cleared. The Finance representative said simply that he had no comments.

"Finally, what is the Police Commissioner's opinion on this case?" the Chairman asked.

"We should send the container back to Rotterdam for further investigation of the whole supply chain. What I mean with the supply chain is the whole chain from Customs declarations in Rotterdam, where the material was merged and with all financial transactions. This is a major undertaking and we should not get involved in that activity," Catherine said. All the people in the conference room nodded to confirm their support for Catherine's proposal. Catherine continued.

"We have done our part in the container content analysis, we have found the use of the content, we have stopped the container and now we return it to the last point of Customs clearance. We still have our own part in this and that is the two men killed in connection with this. This is my opinion, Mr. Chairman," Catherine said.

"I have noted that there is no need for me to use my overall ruling vote in this case. For the record, we shall note that this meeting has decided to send the container back to Rotterdam for further investigation by the countries involved in the supply chain, mainly USA, Germany and Europe," the Chairman said and stood up to signal that the meeting was over.

All the Committee members left the conference room but the Chairman walked to Catherine to stop her before she left as well.

"Catherine, I want to talk with you if you have time?" the Chairman asks.

"Of course. Let's go to my office where we can talk," Catherine said and they both walked into her office.

"It's been noted that most of the issues and concerns, in this case, have been handled professionally without any disturbances in our relationship with our allies. Catherine, to put it shortly, you are doing extremely well," the Chairman said.

"Thank you. I'm happy to hear these positive comments. It has been an unusual case for many of us at the Police Force."

"Indeed but Catherine we still have some things to solve."

They both smiled, and the Chairman left the office. Catherine called Alex to inform him about the decision.

"Hi, Catherine, nice to hear from you. Do we have a decision? Send it back to Rotterdam? Well, that is a surprise but I'm happy that we have a decision. I will take care of everything. Thank you for calling, Catherine," Alex hung up the phone and called Amanda. "Amanda, call an all personnel meeting in the conference room right now. The topic is the container decision and the planning forward."

Amanda called all investigators for the meeting at the office. Several investigators were on the way to their missions when they received the call. Finally, all investigators gathered in the conference room but much later than expected. Everybody could see that Alex was irritated about the delay and the need to wait until everyone was back at the office. Alex stood up and started to talk.

"Listen all, we have now a decision for the next step in our container case. The Police Commissioners Committee has decided that the container with the content is going to be sent back to Rotterdam for further investigations by the USA, Germany, and other EU countries. They will trace back the order chain, supply lanes and financial transactions related to this shipment. What we need to do is to pack everything into the container in the same way as we found it. Questions?"

"I think we need to do the reservation of this shipment on a container vessel with the destination Rotterdam. We have never done this before, so do we even have the knowledge on how to do it?" Hamid asked.

"We don't have this competence, but we need to understand it right now through proper training.

I appoint you, Hamid, to build that competence here within the department. You already have access to the Singapore Port's container system, so I guess it's almost half of the work done," Alex said, and everybody started laughing but Hamid did not look happy about the assignment.

"We continue as before. Kevin and Hamid will have everything in the hangar arranged so that the container gets loaded and transported to the port. We still have the murder part to investigate. That's all for now, so let's get this plan going. Questions?" Alex asked.

"Yes. What is the status in the investigation about the men with the tattoos? I have not heard anything for a long time. Is Ajay still responsible?" Kevin asked.

"Ajay is still responsible. Ajay, can you give a little information on where we are on that investigation?" Alex asked with a smile.

"Yes of course. We don't know where both men lived when they visited Singapore; there are no hotel records of them. The fingerprints have not given any additional information on the Russian man and nothing new on the man found in the Bedok Reservoir. The park worker's clothes have been analyzed and particles of gunpowder were found on those clothes. It's now confirmed that the same type of gunpowder was found on the Russian man that was shot at close range. There is no witness to the actual crime in Bedok Town Park," Ajay said.

There were no further questions and everyone left the conference room in silence. Hamid and Kevin walked to their desks.

"I'm worried about the task that we got. I have never done this before. I don't know where to start," Hamid said.

"Remember that Alex never said when we need to be ready with our task. You have also to remember that this is the first time we are doing this kind of activity. The first thing we need to do is to drink a cup of coffee and then write a list for things we need to do and who will be doing it," Kevin said.

"Yes, you are right. You take everything in a so relaxed way, and you are never worried. I'm getting stressed here. Your words are like relaxing music to me," Hamid said and they both laughed and walked into the coffee area.

Kevin was thinking of this new challenge and how to secure the container shipping to Rotterdam when he came to the insight that Hamid was the key to solve this new challenge.

"Hamid, I'm thinking of our plan. I wanted to share that plan with you if you have time," Kevin said.

"Okay, let's do that. Let's take the conference room it's empty right now," Hamid said.

Hamid and Kevin walked into the conference room and Kevin started to draw a timeline on the whiteboard. Ajay entered the conference room.

"Hi, Ajay, how is the murder investigation going?" Hamid asked.

"We are in the same spot, so nothing new. You two are the new stars of this department. It seems that you can solve all the mysteries. I guess Hamid is the brain behind all this?" Ajay said.

Kevin and Hamid were surprised by Ajay's recognition of their work. They had never heard those kinds of words from Ajay before.

"Thank you, but I think it's the new team approach that Alex has implemented. I work closely with Kevin in all matters to solve this case," Hamid said.

"I have noticed that you both have a good relationship with Alex due to your success. So, tell me what's going on right now in your area?" Ajay asked.

"Well, we are right now trying to establish a timeline to secure what needs to be done so that the container is transported safely to Rotterdam," Hamid said.

"It's important to have a realistic time plan for what needs to be done," Ajay said.

"We need a formal reservation on the vessel to Rotterdam. At the receiving destination side, we need to inform the European authorities about the container content and when it's arriving," Kevin said.

"You two are building our new competence area how to handle container shipping," Ajay said laughing and walked out of the conference room.

At the same time, Alex entered the conference room with a cup of coffee in his hand. "I saw that you were in here, so I decided to come in. I hope I am not disturbing. Let me read what you have planned," Alex said and sipping his coffee.

Alex was now reading the time plan in detail to identify the weak spots or missing activities in the plan. Kevin and Hamid were waiting if Alex had any comments or remarks. After a couple of minutes, Alex was ready to make his comments.

"The plan is looking okay. I can't see any weak points in the plan. However, we need to have the riot wagon with armed police inside the riot wagon and a police car parked outside the port gate. I will arrange this part of the plan since special order is needed to engage the riot wagon," Alex said and walked out of the room.

"Great, now we have the plan approved with some improvements. The only thing remaining is to decide who is doing what," Kevin said.

Hamid continued with the container reservation on the vessel and Kevin was to work on the additional security arrangement. They had to present the whole plan in an executive summary to Alex and specifically address those areas that Alex had identified.

"Now, we have the detailed activity plan ready. I'm happy to know what I shall do," Hamid said and started making notes of the plan.

"I will discuss with Alex about the special security arrangement we are planning to use when the container will be transported to the port and when loaded on the vessel," Kevin said. Kevin was putting on his jacket to go home for the day when he saw Ajay sitting in Alex's office talking about something. Ajay was sitting on his chair, but Alex was walking around in the room and talking. He walked by Amanda's desk.

"Good day for you, I have heard. Alex is happy how you have developed the teamwork and it seems to work as planned for you, but I guess not for all," Amanda said nodding her head to Alex's office where Ajay was now sitting.

"You know I'm happy with my new role and I like to work with Hamid. In the beginning, I was skeptic about the proposal but now, I like the idea of teamwork," Kevin said.

"Yes, it's really inspiring to see you together with Hamid in the office."

"If it works like this in the future, then I'm not going to retire at all," Kevin said when he walked out of the office.

Everything was now ready for the transport of the container to the port. The security arrangements were approved by Alex. The plan was to have one police car in front of the truck pulling the container and another police car behind the truck, together with Kevin and Hamid following the transport in a police car at a distance. Everything will happen with the police blue lights switched off to avoid public interest.

———◆———

Chapter

9

The day had finally come when the container was going to be transported from the hangar to the port and loaded on the vessel to Rotterdam. Kevin and Hamid were at the hangar looking at all the container parts spread on the floor.

"Hamid, have you seen the Customs personnel here. We have requested the Customs support to secure that everything is packed in the right wooden box," Kevin said.

"No, I have not seen them. Do you understand the numbers the Customs officers are using to identify every single piece from the container?" Hamid asked holding a piece of plastic pocket file with the identification number.

"No, the numbers must be connected to other numbers on the boxes where they were found, I guess. We are definitely lacking some shipping competence," Kevin said.

Four men dressed in white protective clothing entered into the hangar. They stopped and looked over the hangar floor for a couple of minutes. Hamid could see that they had the Customs seal on the cloths and on the helmets. Kevin and Hamid walked to them to verify that this was the Customs team they were waiting for.

"Good morning, gentlemen. I'm Kevin and this is my colleague, Hamid. We are from the Criminal Investigations Department. I guess you are from the Customs," Kevin said and stepped forward to shake hands with them.

"Yes, we are from the Customs office and we are here to help you with the loading of the container. I can see that our colleges have been here and placed identification numbers on all parts. This makes our work much easier," one of the Customs officers said.

"Welcome. We need your help to put everything into the right box. It must be loaded in the same way as it was packed before we opened it. Your numbering of the parts is a mystery for us," Kevin said.

"Well, it looks complicated when you see it the first time. When you learn it, then you realize the benefit of the numbering," one of the Customs Officers said.

"Let's start the work and feel free to ask questions if you have a problem with anything. Hamid and I will be here at the hangar until all parts are loaded into the container," Kevin said.

The Customs officers started their work and after an hour the first wooden box was closed and loaded into the container. The heavy steel rolls were moved directly into the container with a forklift. Hamid and Kevin helped with the small components that needed to be placed with care into their plastic pockets.

After several hours of work, all the things were now stored in the wooden boxes and loaded into the container. The Customs officers finalized the paperwork with several pages of specifications of each piece loaded into the container.

"We are ready with the loading and our paperwork is also completed. The only thing remaining is that you need to sign each page in this stack of papers," One of the Customs officers said and handed over the stack of documents to Hamid.

"I can't sign these documents. I don't know anything about those strange identification numbers," Hamid said and stepped back holding both of his hands in the air to indicate that he was not going to sign those documents.

The Customs officers and Kevin laughed at Hamid's reaction.

"Don't worry, Hamid, I will sign it," Kevin said and started to sign on all the pages.

The Customs officers closed the container doors and placed the Customs seal on the door to indicate that the content has been customs cleared. It was an international procedure to save time at export handling without opening the container when it's in transit or transshipment. The Custom officers left the hangar with the original signed documents and Kevin kept the copies. Hamid and Kevin were pleased with their work and the only thing remaining now were to arrange the transport to the port. They walked to the hangar Management office and presented themselves as they always must do as Criminal Investigators.

"I'm Kevin from the Criminal Investigation Department and this is my college Hamid," Kevin said and they both showed their Criminal Investigation Department's badges. The hangar clerk looked at the badges carefully before he gave the badges back to them.

"Gentlemen, what can I do for you?" the clerk asked.

"We have a shipping container in the hangar that we need to transport to the port. Can you please release it? One-way container transport to the port is all that we need," Kevin said and showed the clerk the pack of customs documents in his hand.

"Yes, I can arrange it, but you need to fill in this document with some facts about the container content before I can arrange it," The clerk said and handed over the document to Kevin.

Kevin read the document and shook his head. He realized that the information requested in the document was not easy to fill in.

"We have missed something in our planning. It's a lot of information that needs to be filled into this document and I have to say that I don't know the answers. It's been a long day and it's getting late I think it would be best to do this tomorrow instead," Kevin said looking at his watch.

Hamid nodded to the proposal after looking at the document shortly. They left the hangar Management office with a relief to handle the information requested the next day instead.

The next morning Kevin and Hamid were early to the office to finalize the paperwork for the transport that was requested. Kevin picked up the document and started to read it.

"It's very complicated for us to fill this because we are not a commercial organization, we are a Government organization. The questions in the document are not made for our criminal investigation activities. This transport is a part of an ongoing criminal investigation," Kevin said.

At the same time Alex entered the office and Kevin waved to him to come to his desk. Alex observed Kevin's waving and walked to him.

"Hi, Kevin, how is everything going at the hangar?" Alex asked.

"All the contents were properly loaded, and the container was sealed by the Customs. That activity went smoothly without any problems. But to transport the container to the port seems to be a major issue. Look at this document that we need to fill in before we can start the transport to the port," Kevin said and handed over the document to Alex.

Alex read the document and he also started to shake his head. After the first few questions, he realized the difficulty to answer them correctly.

"I understand this is very complicated and the requested information in this document is not made for the situation we are handling now. We need expertise in the export area to help us with this document. I will talk to Amanda if she knows who can do this for us. She also knows the history why we are in this situation to export the container back to Rotterdam," Alex said and walked to Amanda with the document.

Kevin was smiling and looking at Alex when he walked to Amanda. He seemed to be so happy about the situation.

"I can't remember the last time when this has happened to me. I'm surprised that Alex did it. It's almost time that I start to believe in humanity again," Kevin said and started to read the daily newspaper.

Hamid was looking at Kevin and wondered what he meant by saying that. He did not understand the meaning of Kevin's comment.

"Kevin, I don't understand. What had Alex done that has this effect?"

"That my boss takes over my work and carries it to another person. My experience is that it's done the other way around," Kevin said with a smile.

They both laughed at Kevin's comments. They felt relieved over the fact that the document was now handled by Amanda.

After lunch, Amanda walked to Kevin with the document, with all fields correctly filled in. "Here, Kevin,

Alex told me that you are the receiver of this document. It's now filled in by our special department together with the Customs office of course. I hope it is okay for you?"

Kevin stood up and took the document in his hand and gave Amanda a big hug.

"Amanda, you save my day with this. I'm glad that you are around. I would have never done it myself even if I had worked on it for a week," Kevin said.

Amanda was looking at Kevin with big eyes and surprised over his nice words. It was most unusual for Kevin to act and express himself in this way.

"What has happened to him?" Amanda said looking at Hamid and pointing at Kevin.

"It's a long story, Amanda, but your support came just in time when he needed it the most," Hamid said.

"Hamid, let's have lunch and it's going to be the 'ala carte' menu today. We have done a great job and we are ready to transport the container to the port," Kevin said and they both left the office for lunch.

After lunch, they went back to the hangar Management center to arrange the transport with the document correctly filled in now.

"Here is the document filled in and ready," Kevin said and handed over the document to the clerk.

"The documents are good for the transport. I have a truck available in about one hour. Do you want to take it, or do you want to wait until tomorrow?" the clerk asked.

"We take it today and right away," Kevin said.

"Sorry, but I can now see that one important information is missing in your document and that is the destination address where the container is going to be transported," the clerk said and handed over the document to Kevin.

Kevin realized that he needed to call the Port Master directly to get the address. He also informed him that the container will be delivered to the port later today.

"The container shall be delivered to the Brani Terminal Gate 2," Kevin said to the clerk.

"The documents are good now. You are now ready for the transport so please go and wait outside the hangar door. The truck will be there shortly," the clerk said and walked away from the desk.

Kevin and Hamid walked the short distance to the hangar and waited for the truck outside the hangar door. They had also asked for two police cars to escort the truck to the port. The truck arrived, and the truck started to load the container on the trailer. Kevin showed the driver with his hand that he could start the transportation. They were now on the way with one police car driving in front of the truck, the other was following the truck and after that Kevin and Hamid were following in a police car. No sirens or blue lights were used to not attract the public interest in the transport.

They arrived at the terminal and the Port Master was waiting for them at the gate. The truck drove directly into the container area through the gates, but the Police cars stopped outside the gate itself. Kevin and Hamid stepped out from the police car to meet the Port Master.

"Gentlemen, welcome. Here are your badges and you need to wear them inside the port at all times," Port Master said.

"Thank you. I'm glad that the container is on the way without any hassle," Kevin said with a smile.

"Let's go and check the container. I will show you where it is. We will take my car with the official port logo," the Port Master said.

They drove into the huge container storage area. There were a lot of containers in several layers stacked on top of each other. Between the containers, there were roads like streets where the trucks were driving. The containers were making walls on each periphery.

"Here it is... the famous container," the Port Master said.

The container was placed alone with no other containers loaded on top of it. This was done to ensure a fast loading to the vessel.

"Yes, the correct identification number SCNU3604628 is there. I have had the identification number in my head for a long time," Hamid said, and they all laughed at Hamid's comment.

"The Customs seal is in place and unbroken. Everything is ready to load the container. We will start the loading of the vessel tomorrow and your container is planned to be loaded shortly after lunch time," the Port Master said.

"We will be here before lunch tomorrow," Kevin said.

They all traveled back to the terminal gate and home for the day. Everything was now ready for the final step, which was to load the container on the vessel. This remaining step seemed to be easy. Kevin and Hamid were pleased with the progress so far.

The next morning Kevin arrived early in the office and he was the first person there that morning. He felt like a young investigator who had succeeded in doing something for the first time. Amanda arrived and was surprised to see Kevin sitting on his desk. She walked to him.

"Kevin, what has happened? You are here so early today. I have not seen this kind of motivation from you for years," Amanda said.

"Well, sometimes good things happen and now it has happened to me," Kevin said with a smile.

"What has happened that is making you so happy? Tell me more," Amanda said

"We have finalized our mission to transport the container to the port without any issues. It was teamwork between me and Hamid. Of course, with your valuable help in filling the crazy document for the transport, Amanda," Kevin explained.

"I'm happy for your success and you need to report this to Alex. He needs to listen to your success story," Amanda said.

"I will wait until Hamid has arrived in the office. I want to meet Alex together with him. You know teamwork," Kevin said.

"You have really got it; the teamwork spirit, Kevin," Amanda said laughing and walked to her desk.

Hamid arrived at the office, but he was tired and not in so good mood. Kevin could see that when he didn't turn on his computers directly as he arrived. He was only sitting and watching his black displays without saying anything.

"Hamid, we are successful together. We have done our transport mission perfectly without any incidents. That is what I call teamwork. What do you think about that?" Kevin asked.

"I'm a computer guy and I don't feel I can contribute a lot in the fieldwork activities. Out in the field, you face the unknown and I'm not so good at improvising. I'm thinking that perhaps I don't have the right profile to work out in the field."

"Listen, Hamid, you are doing great. In fact, better than I was doing at your age. Most of us have a tough start. This is one of the most challenging departments with high requirements on the persons who jump into this. You have the right profile, Hamid. You are not afraid to take on new challenges and above all your computer skills have helped us several times already. We need you here, Hamid."

Kevin could see that Alex had arrived in his office. Sometimes there was a morning queue outside his office but not this morning. Amanda waved to Kevin to tell him he can walk into Alex's office.

Kevin stood up and waved to Amanda that he was going to Alex's office.

"Hamid, follow me. We are going to visit Alex in his office."

Hamid followed Kevin without asking why. Kevin knocked on the door and walked in with Hamid.

"Alex, good morning. Do you have time for our report about the container transport?" Kevin asked.

"Great. I saw that both of you are back at the office so everything is done now. Right?" Alex asked.

"Yes, everything is done according to the plan. The container is at the port, now ready to be loaded onto the vessel and transported to Rotterdam. The actual loading will happen today in the afternoon, so we are going there soon. Hamid has made all the necessary arrangements with the shipping agents."

"Gentlemen, I must say that you have done this extremely well. Good luck for the afternoon with the final loading. Hamid, you have contributed to this department very much in just a couple of months and I'm proud of you," Alex said.

Kevin and Hamid walked out from Alex office with big smiles on their faces. Everybody at the office could see that the meeting with Alex had been a good one.

"Thank you, Kevin, I really needed this feedback. Now I can feel the motivation coming back for the field work," Hamid said.

"What we need now is a steady lunch before we travel to the port," Kevin said and they both walked out from the office smiling. When they passed Amanda's desk she gave them a thumbs up.

After lunch, they drove to the port to see the actual loading of the container. Kevin and Hamid arrived at the port in a police car and they could see the Port Master standing in front of the gate waiting for them.

"Gentlemen, welcome. There is the vessel that will take the container to Rotterdam. You can see that loading of containers is ongoing," Port Master said and pointed at the vessel with his hand.

"Wow! It's huge when you stand close to it. I have seen these vessels from a distance but never so close," Hamid said.

It was a gigantic container vessel with several layers of containers on the deck. Several cranes were loading and offloading the containers. Trucks were also driving around the cranes and between the containers.

The Port Master's main tool was the handheld radio that he used to talk to his staff in the port. When he pushed the call all function button, then all personnel in the port can listen and talk to him directly. This function gave everybody in the port the possibility to get a fast answer from the right person. The Port Master started to speak in his handheld radio, and he pressed the speak all button.

"Hi, all in the port. The Port Master here. How much time do we have until the container with the ID SCNU3604628 will be loaded on the vessel?" the Port Master asked in his handheld radio.

After a short time of silence, a voice answered in the handheld radio. "Loading is planned to start in about three hours," the radio voice said.

"Gentlemen, I guess you heard that we have three hours before they start to load the container," the Port Master said.

"You have a very good function in the handheld radio that you can contact all personnel directly by pressing this one button only," Hamid said and pointed at the button.

"Yes. It's a matter of security also to give fast information about risky situations to all in the port so they can take action if needed," Port Master said. "Would you like to have some coffee while we are waiting?" Port Master asked.

"That would be great, thank you," Kevin said.

They all jumped into the Port Master's car and he drove to the building where the coffee area was located. They all walked to the coffee area.

"I will leave you two here in the coffee area for a short while. I need to take care of some urgent business, but I will be back shortly," Port Master said and left Kevin and Hamid.

At the coffee area, there were a lot of shipping magazines on the table. There were also a couple of truck drivers drinking coffee and waiting for some paperwork to be ready. Hamid started to read one of the magazines and Kevin was walking around with his cup of coffee in his hand. Kevin was watching out from the coffee area window to check if riot wagon and the police car was parked outside the main gate. The riot wagon was there but not the police car, so he decided to call Alex.

"Hi, Alex, Kevin here. I'm at the port now with Hamid to check the container loading. I can see the riot wagon, but I can't see the police car that was ordered to be outside the main gate."

"Let me check what has happened. When is the container going to be loaded?"

"The loading will start in about three hours," Alex said.

"Okay, Kevin. Then we have time to investigate this. I will also put some additional police resources on standby in case we need them with short notice," Alex said.

"That sounds like a good idea Alex," Kevin said.

□□□

After a couple of minutes Alex called Kevin back and he answered immediately.

"Hi, Kevin. The police car is on the way. They have been parked outside the wrong gate," Alex said.

"Good then we are ready," Kevin said.

After a couple of minutes, the police car arrived at the gate. The riot wagon and the police care were now parked outside the gate where they had a full view of all the lanes that went in and out from the port terminal. Kevin was amazed by the effective handling of the containers and how they kept track of all movements of the containers. The Port Master walked into the coffee area and pressed some buttons on the coffee machine. Kevin walked to him, but he could not see Hamid around.

"Where, is Hamid?" Kevin asked the Port Master.

"I met him outside with one of our computer guys. I guess he is interested in the computer system that we use to run the port. We have one of the most advanced computer systems in the world," Port Master said.

"I knew he had to check your systems; it must be advanced when you are handling huge number of containers round the clock. You know Hamid is our computer specialist and he brings new type of investigation competence," Kevin said.

"I know. We have also hired young people with that competence. Without them, we would not be in the business."

"Is it possible for me to take a walk inside the port area? The weather is nice and it would be good to stretch my legs."

"Yes, you can do that, but I recommend you take one of our hand-held radio units with you. You can reach all personnel when you push this button. You can also listen to others when they talk. That function can be useful if you get lost in the container jungle," The Port Master said and they both were laughing.

Kevin was looking at the handheld radio and he pushed the call all button. He could now listen to the port personnel talk. He did not understand what they said as they used abbreviations and numbers in their conversation.

Kevin walked out from the coffee area with his handheld radio unit in his hand.

"Be careful of the trucks. They are always in a hurry and they are not used to have people walking around in the port area," the Port Master said.

"I will," Kevin said and walked out to the container area.

The Port Master was right about the trucks that were speeding in the area. Some of the trucks had a container loaded and some of them without any load. There were hundreds of containers in different sizes and trucks in different colors. The containers were loaded three or four on top of each other. Kevin's mobile was ringing, and he answered. It was Hamid calling.

"Hi, Hamid. I'm outside the coffee area, just walking around. If you'll look out from the cafeteria window, then you can see me. I will wave to you," Kevin said and waved to the direction of the coffee area.

"I can see you now, so wait I will come out and join you," Hamid said.

After a couple of minutes, Hamid joined Kevin and they walked together in the port. They discussed the case and how unusual it was with several strange findings. When Kevin and Hamid reached an intersection at the port, Hamid lifted his hand to stop Kevin from walking. Hamid was pointing with his hand to a truck that was slowly moving forward. Both men stopped walking.

"This can't be true, I must be dreaming this," Hamid said with a whispering voice.

Kevin was looking at Hamid and wondering what he meant.

"Kevin, can you see what I see?"

"No, I can't see so tell me what you see," Kevin said and started looking around in different directions.

"Look at the truck in front of us; can you see the container numbers? It's our container."

"I see the truck, but I can't see the container numbers; it's too far away."

"I'm reading SCNU3604628. Those characters are sitting on that container truck in front of us. Same container ID we have on our container," Hamid said in a high voice.

"It's not possible... it can't be. Something is totally wrong. We have to stop that truck and talk to the driver," Hamid said and pointed at the truck in front of him.

The truck was forced to stop and let another truck pass in front of it. Now Kevin saw an opportunity to reach the truck. He started to run as fast as he could while Hamid tried to stop him. Hamid started to run after Kevin, but he could not catch up with him.

"Kevin, please wait… wait," Hamid shouted but Kevin continued to run. He could not hear Hamid. He was totally focused on reaching the truck before it started to move again. Kevin almost fell onto the gravel, but he managed to reach the truck and to show his police badge to the driver. The truck was moving forward slowly but then it stopped. Hamid had to stop running to catch his breath. He was definitely not in good shape.

He could see Kevin at a distance when he opened the driver's door slowly. Suddenly there was gunfire and Hamid could see Kevin falling backward from the truck to the ground. Kevin was shot by someone in the truck.

"No, no. Kevin, please don't let this happen to you. Shit!" Hamid shouted as he was running as fast as he could again.

The truck door closed slowly, and the truck started to speed off. When Hamid reached Kevin, he could see the handheld radio was lying in Kevin's open hand. Hamid could hear somebody talking into the radio unit, so he shouted into it.

"Officer down... Officer down at the port. Send reinforcements and ambulance. Block all exits at the port… block all exists," Hamid screamed in the handheld radio in a desperate hope that somebody in the port could hear him.

Hamid was lucky the call all button was pressed in the handheld radio so all personnel at the port could hear his desperate screaming for help. Kevin had somehow managed to push the call-all button when he was slipping onto the ground. Shortly after Hamid's message, there was a voice in the radio saying, "All trucks... all trucks officer shot at the port. Block all port exits with all you have," The radio crackled and died.

Hamid recognized that it was the Port Master's voice. He had heard Hamid's scream for help.

Kevin was laying on his back on the ground without moving or talking. Hamid could see that blood was now pouring through his shirt. Hamid tried to talk to Kevin and trying to ignore all the blood on his hand. Kevin was bleeding profusely and Hamid felt very helpless in the situation.

———◆———

Chapter

10

"Kevin, take it easy, man. The ambulance is on its way you will make it. Don't worry and don't move," Hamid said.

The riot wagon and the police car that was parked outside the gate arrived at the scene in a cloud of dust. The riot wagon stopped at a distance to check the surroundings if there were any other threats close to the scene, but the police officer jumped out from his car.

"What has happened?" the policeman asked.

"Kevin was shot by someone from a truck. The truck is still inside the port and we need to stop it. Call for reinforcements," Hamid said at the same time holding up Kevin's head with his hand and trying to stop the blood flow from his chest.

The policeman jumped into his car and called for reinforcement.

"All units... all units, we have an officer shot from a truck here at the port. The suspected truck is still inside the port. We need reinforcements to block all exits. I repeat officer shot... block all exits in the port," the policeman said in the car radio.

Several trucks and forklifts were now parked in front of all exits, blocking ingoing and outgoing traffic. They had heard the Port Master's call to block the exits with all they have and so they did. The drivers had stepped out from the trucks and were now discussing in small groups what had happened. The policeman walked back to Hamid to get a description of the suspected truck. Hamid informed him about the container number. The policeman communicated the description on his radio.

"All units, I have the container ID numbers SCNU3604628. This is the container that the truck is pulling. The driver is armed and dangerous. There can be several more armed persons in the truck. The location of the truck is unknown, but it's still inside the port and all exit gates are blocked," the policeman said on his radio.

The ambulance arrived, and the police helped the ambulance personnel to load Kevin into the ambulance. Hamid was standing shocked and passively watching when the ambulance and the police car drove away with the stress sirens and blue lights. Hamid was now standing alone between the containers. Nobody asked Hamid if he wanted to jump into the ambulance or the Police car. The riot wagon was now driving slowly around in the area in search of the truck. Both the police car and the Ambulance were gone. Hamid realized that he was in a dangerous situation.

Hamid could hear the helicopter's blades at a distance. He could see heavy armed police running between the containers. He thought that he was wearing civil clothes and he could be mistaken as one of the suspects. Hamid tried to find his way back to the main gate, but all the containers looked the same, so he knew he was lost.

He was shaking by the shock of what had happened to Kevin and he felt the need to rest. He decided to slowly sit down on the gravel behind a container. The scary thing for him was that it could have happened to him if he had opened the truck door. He could now hear a helicopter hovering closer than before and that was worrying to him. Suddenly, he heard a loudspeaker voice behind him from a distance saying.

"Give up! You are surrounded by armed police," the loudspeaker voice at the helicopter said.

Then there was silence couple of seconds and then heavy gunfire started. Hamid was looking up to see what was going on. He could see the helicopter flying away from the gunfire sound. Suddenly, he could hear a truck engine start and it was very close as only a couple of containers were between him and the truck. He needed to move to a safer place to avoid being detected by the people in the truck. He spotted a narrow space between the two containers that looked safe for him, so he pushed himself in between the two containers. He could see the riot wagon slowly drive by his hiding place, but he was afraid to move and reveal his hiding place. Now the truck engine stopped, and all was silent. Hamid moved slowly to the corner of the container to see where the truck was.

The riot wagon spotted Hamid when he was looking out from behind the container. They called to him through the loudspeaker system.

"You there lay down with your hands behind your head," the voice said.

Hamid lay down slowly on the ground with his hands behind his head. A group of the heavily armed police was now walking slowly to him with all their weapons pointing at him. Hamid understood that he was in a high-risk situation and his smallest mistake might let him get shot by the police. He had read of those cases when nervous policemen open fire by mistake in a stressful situation.

"Don't shoot... don't shoot! I'm a police officer. I have a badge and I can show you," Hamid screamed in panic.

The riot police did not answer. They continue to walk slowly against Hamid with the weapons pointing at him. Everything was now silent; no truck sound or chopper sound. The only thing Hamid could hear was the police heavy boots crushing the gravel on the road. Now he could hear a voice close behind his back. "Don't move. I will search you for an id," the voice said.

One of the policemen searched him and the others were standing in a distance with pointing weapons at him. When the police found Hamid's police badge he got more relaxed.

"Sorry, sir. I can now see that you are a police officer so please stand up," The policeman said smiling and signaled with his hand to the other policemen to lower their guns.

Hamid stood up and brushed his clothes. He was also smiling and felt embarrassed over the situation he was in.

"Thank you, I was nervous over to be shot by mistake. Anyhow, I'm glad that you are here," Hamid said.

"You should be nervous and scared. It's not normal that a police officer is hiding behind a container in a hostile environment like this," the policeman said and all the riot police standing around Hamid laughed at the situation.

Hamid and all the heavily armed policemen jumped into the riot wagon and rolled again slowly between the containers. Hamid explained to the police the whole story from the beginning when Kevin was shot to his hiding place behind a container. Suddenly, there were some shots hitting the riot wagon. The men inside could hear the metallic sound when the bullets hit the outside armor. The riot wagon driver accelerated to escape from the gunfire. The riot wagon stopped between two containers and the men regrouped to defend themselves. One group of the riot police was now watching the back side of the wagon and one group was watching the area in front of the wagon. The driver remained in the driving seat prepared to a fast rollout from the situation. Suddenly, there was a message from the police radio.

"All units, all units... there is a police officer missing inside the port area. We don't know if he is taken hostage or alive. His name is Hamid Munsi. Try to locate him in the port area," the radio message said.

The policeman that searched Hamid was smiling as he recognized the name. He picked up the microphone and communicated the good news to all the units.

"All units, all units, we have found him. He is riding in our wagon now. He is alive and well," the policeman said and all the riot police in the wagon were happy to be the ones that found Hamid. Hamid's mobile was ringing, and he could see that it was Alex, so he answered immediately.

"Hi, Alex. I'm sitting in the riot wagon with heavily armed policemen. Yes, I'm okay and safe. Is Kevin OK? So, the operation is ongoing right now. I hope he gets well soon," Hamid said with a nervous voice.

Hamid was nervous to be trapped in the riot wagon and to be shot at so he was eager to leave the dangerous place.

"Alex, what shall I do I'm stuck here in this riot wagon?" Hamid asked.

"Ask the group manager in the wagon to drive you to the gate if that is okay with you?" Alex asked.

"That would be a great relief, Alex," Hamid said and all the riot police in the wagon laughed.

The riot wagon drove slowly to the harbor gate and Hamid jumped into the police car and soon he was on his way to the office. The riot police were in full attention all the time because they did not know where the truck was. They could again hear the police radio call for attention.

"All units, all units, the truck is still inside the port area. The truck's location is unknown. All units inside the port park all vehicles now. No vehicle movements inside the port area. The helicopter will start the air search for the container," the radio voice said.

They could now hear the helicopter sound at distance. Suddenly, there was heavy gunfire and this time it was several guns firing altogether. This time the gunfire was so intense, it sounded like in a war zone.

"My God. It seems there are several guns that are firing and it's not our guns because they don't sound like that. This time big caliber machine guns were involved," one policeman said.

The police radio sent a message again. "All units, all units, the helicopter has been shot down by heavy machine guns. It was counted at most three individuals exited from the truck and they were all firing at the helicopter. Hold your positions and no vehicle movements in the port. There can be more people inside the truck. The helicopter has made an emergency landing outside the port area. The police in the helicopter is not injured. The emergency landing was made to assess the damages on the helicopter. Stay put all units," the message said and everybody in the riot wagon was happy to hear that no policemen were killed or wounded in the helicopter.

When Hamid arrived at the office he noted a chaotic scene. All police resources were now engaged in the port incident. Hamid sat down in his chair and stared at his black display screens. Alex walked to his desk.

"Hamid I'm glad you are okay and you did well today. I can understand that you are still a little bit shocked by the incident," Alex said.

"What about Kevin's condition?" Hamid asked.

"He will survive, and he is right now sleeping deeply after the operation. We were lucky that it was a small caliber handgun that was used. He should have had his bulletproof vest for this work. I know it sounds like an overreaction to carry that for an administrative task in the port. But it is necessary."

"I'm glad that he is okay. I really want to visit him when it's possible to do so."

Hamid was looking at the floor. Alex could see that Hamid was still shocked after the event. Alex had been exposed to that danger several times, so he knew of Hamid's present psychological status.

"Hamid, you can go home and rest. We can discuss more tomorrow," Alex said.

Hamid nodded and walked slowly to the door. All personnel in the office were looking at Hamid when he walked out of the office. They were all aware of what had happened in the port. Alex decided to call all investigators to an urgent meeting in the conference room. He began to understand that the port situation was not going to be a police matter for much longer. All investigators were now in the conference room when Alex started to speak.

"Welcome. I want to inform you that Kevin is okay after the operation but still weak and needs to rest. We have sent him some flowers and hopefully, we can visit him soon. We have decided to hold our ground at the port with no offensive activities from our side. Our strategy now is to maintain a standoff situation until any further notice. They are trapped inside the harbor and they can't escape. Any questions?" Alex asked.

"How long will the standoff last? We have to do something?" one investigator asked.

"I have talked to the Police Commissioner and there will be an emergency meeting with the board tonight. They will decide how to proceed," Alex said.

The meeting was over, and the investigators left the room. At the same time, at the port, there was a strong explosion that vibrated windows far away from the port. A couple of minutes later Alex's mobile was ringing and so did many other phones in the office. Everybody knew something happened.

Alex picked his phone and answered. It was the Port Manager screaming on the phone.

"Hi Alex. It's me; the Port Manager. They have blown one of our cranes and the crane has now fallen into the sea," the Port Manager screamed.

"Calm down and take it from the beginning," Alex said.

"We have turned off all the lights in the harbor. In the cover of the dark, they had placed a bomb on one of the crane legs and they detonated it. When the crane's leg was gone the whole crane had now fallen into the sea," the Port Manager said.

"My God, this is bad news. I need to inform the Police Commissioner about this. I'll inform the further plan once finalized," Alex said.

Alex called the Police Commissioner and the secretary answered.

"The Commissioner is at a meeting. She cannot be disturbed," the secretary said.

"I'm Alex Hen, the Head of the Criminal Investigation Department and I need to talk to the Commissioner at once. It's an emergency," Alex said in a high voice.

"Oh, it's you, Alex, sorry. Yes, she told me that if you call she will take the call. I will pass her a note. She is in a meeting right now. Hang on the phone. I am sure she will come and talk to you," the secretary said.

The secretary entered the ongoing meeting and passed a note to Catherine. She read it shortly and left the meeting room to pick up the phone. "Hi, Alex. What's the news?"

"They have now detonated a bomb at the port. The bomb was strapped to one of the crane legs and then detonated. The crane fell into the sea, but nobody was hurt. Now we know they have this capability. This was done when all lights were shut off at the port."

"What's the status of one of your man who was shot at the port today. Sorry, what was his name again?"

"Kevin... His name is Kevin and he is a very experienced investigator of my team. I use him mainly as our 'Senior Advisor' and he is an important person in my team. He has been operated on and the bullet was removed so he will be okay. It was a small caliber handgun so the damage from the bullet was not so critical."

"Thank you, Alex, for calling. I will inform at the Committee meeting about this new development. I want you also to be here as a standby for support in case they want to have more detailed information about the status at the port. We will have the meeting today at 9pm. Can you be here?" Catherine asked.

"It's seven pm right now. No problem; I can be there on time," Alex said.

Alex was happy about it as he was never called to be a standby person at the Commissioner's Committee meeting. This was a great recognition of his achievements in the police force coming in a very critical time. He rushed home to take a shower, change the shirt and polish his shoes. He was dedicated to look the best and do the best he could in this great opportunity for advancement.

PART FIVE

The Operation

Chapter

11

The Police Commissioner Committee members were now gathered in the conference room. The tension was high and informal discussions were going on between the members. They were all waiting for the Chairman to enter the meeting. Alex was also called to the meeting to support Catherine if the members wanted to have more detailed information about the port situation. He was sitting outside the conference room ready to come in if he was called for.

Finally, the Police Commissioner and the Chairman entered the conference room. All discussions stopped at once when they could see that a General from the Army joined the meeting. When all the members and the General had taken their seats, the chairman opened the meeting.

"Welcome to this emergency meeting. I guess we all know what we have on the agenda. You have all noticed that we have invited an external participant to cover the agenda topic. The expert is the General of the Army's Special Operations Task Force. We all welcome Mr. Kenny Tong to this meeting as his views on this topic are very important," the Chairman said.

The General was of around sixty years of age with gold plated glasses. He was dressed in full uniform and he was wearing several types of military decorations of unknown origin. He was in good physical condition for his age. His appearance was strong, and the body language and voice were decisive.

The Chairman looked around the table and opened the meeting.

"Welcome Committee members. We will now start our meeting by letting the Police Commissioner present actual status at the Port. Please, Catherine," the Chairman said and nodded to Catherine at the same time.

"Thank you, Mr. Chairman. Maybe we now have to handle a heavily armed terrorist group and not an ordinary criminal street gang. In summary, we have one officer shot and wounded at the hospital right now. We have all the exits blocked and we have also taken actions to prevent people and vessels to leave or enter the harbor area. All harbor personnel has now been evacuated from the port to prevent a hostage situation. We don't know the number of armed persons we are facing. We have seen three armed men open fire. But there can be more terrorists hiding inside the container. We have not been able to identify the terrorist's nationalities or what they want. The riot police are holding their position inside the harbor. The situation can be described as a standoff. However, I have received information a couple of hours ago that they have blown up one of our container cranes. This is an escalation from their side. Any questions?" Catherine asked.

The conference room was silent. The members watched the General, to see if he had something to say, but he was only making notes and did not say anything. Then the Commissioner Committee Chairman continued, "Thank you Catherine for the introduction. We can all agree that the situation is critical and that special actions must now be taken and fast," the Chairman said looking at the General to indicate that he should say something.

"Mr. Chairman, can I have the word?" the General asked, and the Chairman nodded for acceptance.

The General stood up and started to walk around in the room with his hands behind his back. The members could all see that he was thinking deeply to select the right words.

"Members. What we are facing here is a hijack situation of our important trading ground. Important infrastructure has also now been destroyed and I want to classify this as an act of war. This group has now attacked our people and property for some reason, but we don't know why. They are now driving around in our territory with a container consisting of parts to build an intercontinental missile with the capability to carry nuclear warheads. We don't know if they have something more hiding inside the container," the General said.

The members were whispering to each other while the General was walking around in the conference room not saying anything. Then the General continued, "I want to inform you all in this Committee that I have full approval from our Government to use military force to solve this," the General said standing behind the Chairman. The members were looking at each other without saying anything.

"This means that this is not a police matter anymore and the Army will take over all operations in the port?" the Chairman asked.

"Yes, Mr. Chairman, that is correct. However, I would need police support. After all, the police forces are now holding the standoff as we speak and that is a good thing," the General said.

"Will any deadly force be used to solve this?" one of the members asked.

"I know that the police have already given them an offer to surrender but without acceptance from their side. The Army will also give them a second offer to surrender. If the second offer to surrender is not accepted by them as well, then the deadly forces will be used without any hesitation," the General said.

"Is there an option to take them alive and interrogate them?" Another from the members asked.

The general raised his voice and was looking sharply to the member who asked. "What we have now is an attack on vital Singapore infrastructure, property and personnel, by blowing up cranes in our port. We have the deadly force ready. I see this as an act of war and a hijacking of our territory," the General said and continued.

"We have no idea how much power they hold or back up they have. We don't know if they have a lot of ammo, what are their military skills and what their motive is. All we know, members, that we can't let the dangerous situation continue much longer," the General said.

"Do we know if they are Singapore citizens?" one member asked.

"We don't know their nationalities. There is nothing that points to any specific group," Catherine said.

"Will the deadly force be used even if they have Singapore citizenship?" one member asked.

"Let me remind you all where we are right now. We are in a grey area of war and not war. This is not a war against any country. It's a war against an unknown enemy that wants to destroy everything we have built up since 1965. We have the right to defend our infrastructure and all people that want to live here in peace. So, anybody who is part of the plan of hijacking our infrastructure is first an enemy of our country and later citizen of the same," the General said.

"How will this be received by the outside world that we are killing people and using our army and that too without a firm trail?" one of the members asked.

"We are trying to defend ourselves against an unknown group of people who have shot a police officer, shot on the riot wagon. We will give them a firm option to surrender without conditions. If they open fire at my men, well then, we fire back with all we have and that is going to be deadly, of course," General said.

The conference room was silent, and the General's speech had made an impression to those who hesitated to use the Army in this case. The Chairman and the Police Commissioner have had a pre-meeting talk with the General and his staff before the actual Committee meeting, so they were fully informed of what would happen at the meeting.

The Chairman stood up from his chair and started to walk around in the conference room and that was unusual. Then he stopped walking and was standing still and watching at all the members.

"Members, we have now heard Catherine about the present situation at the port. We have also heard the General's view on this matter. The General has communicated that he has the full authority to take over, and by military means, they'll lead the port operation. This authority is given by a signed order from the Government. Based on these facts the formal decision is easy. We formally here and now decide to hand over the responsibility to the Army. The handover date is today, and time will be noted in the minutes after this meeting. Any questions or opinions before this decision?" the Chairman asked.

All members shook their heads to indicate that they did not have any questions. The members left the conference room without discussion. The Committee Chairman waved at Catherine to indicate that he wanted to talk to her. Catherine walked slowly to the Chairman and the Chairman waited until all members had left the room.

"Catherine, I know we are doing the right thing to let this go to the army and we are also released from the responsibility. We don't have the firepower that is needed for this case," Chairman said.

"I agree and support the decision. Our firepower will not match what is needed in this case. I have one demand and that we have our Police force in the port and they are going to be part of the operation."

"Continue... I do hope that I can fulfill it."

"My demand is that the Head of the Criminal Investigation Department Mr. Alex Hen can participate in the planning and be fully involved in the execution. I have my Police still involved so that would be a fair request," Catherine said.

"I think your request can be accepted and I support it. I will talk to the General about this," the Chairman said.

Catherine smiled and nodded to the Chairman when she walked out of the conference room.

She noticed that Alex was still sitting outside the conference room, so she asked Alex to come to her office to inform him about the decision. At the same time, the Chairman called the General.

"Hi, Mr. Tong, it's Mr. Lok the Committee Chairman. I have received a request that I want to discuss with you," the Chairman said.

"Yes. I have always time if you are calling. What is it?" The General asked.

"Well, it's our Police Commissioner. She wants one of the top managers from the Criminal Investigation Department to participate in your planning and in the execution at the port. I support her in this request. After all, we have our police force engaged at the port right now."

There was a long silence before the General answered.

"Well, you are right that the police are engaged, and I need them there for my planning. Okay, let's fulfill her request. What is his name?" the General asked.

"Great decision. His name is Alex Hen and I will inform Catherine about this so he can plan for this," the Chairman said.

The Chairman called Catherine and she answered directly when she saw who it was.

"Yes, Catherine here. Well, that is good news. I will inform Alex directly about it and in fact, that is easy because he is sitting in my office right now," Catherine said and hung up.

"I have good news for you, Alex. It's going to be most exciting for you. I had asked the Army if you can be a part of the Army's planning of the operation and the full operation at the port," Catherine said with a smile.

Alex was surprised about the possibility and honored by the opportunity; a little bit scared also to face terrorists that can be deadly from so close.

"That will be interesting. This is extremely important to my men to have complete information about what actions are according to plan and what actions are not," Alex said.

"Good. Any news from the port?" Catherine asked.

"No news. We are holding our standoff and we have a good view of the truck. It's not moving. We have also switched on the lights in the harbor after the crane bomb. Kevin's situation is now stable," Alex said.

"Great. The Army is now responsible for the operation."

"I support the decision. We are dealing with a heavily armed group and we don't know what capabilities they have," Alex said and left the office for home.

◻◻◻

It was 11pm and the port was now fully bathing in lights and the police units were standing still at their places. All employees had been evacuated. The only port personnel remaining in the port was the Port Master and he was sitting inside the riot wagon.

The night shift personnel started to arrive at the port. They were all stopped by the police from entering the port. Also, international reporters with camera teams had arrived and were stopped by the police when they wanted to get closer to the port gates. They requested comments from authorities about the situation and the planning of actions. A formal press release was issued by the Police Commissioner Catherine Zheng.

"The planning to solve the port incident is now ongoing together with several authorities including the army. There are no demands put forward from the terrorists. We have no knowledge of how many they are and what they represent. We will communicate in more details when we have more information. Until then, it will be best if the civilians stay away from the area."

———◆———

Chapter

12

The Army's Special Operation Task Force Officers were gathered in the conference room at the Armed Forces Bedok Camp II. The participants were from the Army, Air Force, and the Navy. General Kenny Tong was opening the meeting and he was now serving as the 'Commander and Chief' of the whole operation. The General opened the meeting.

"Alright, this is the walkthrough of our strategy to end the port occupation. We have with us the key people from several military branches that have developed the strategy. I guess most of you have noticed a civil participant in the meeting. Let me introduce you to the Head of the Criminal Investigation Department, Mr. Alex Hen. His people will be holding the standoff at the port until we arrive. The suspects are heavily armed, and the Police can't meet their firepower. That's why; this is now a military operation. Any comments from Mr.Hen?" the General asked.

Alex stood up to speak. "I'm thankful for your support in this critical situation. The police orders are to prevent any person or vehicle to enter the port area, hold the standoff and not to take any offensive actions. The suspects have also destroyed one of the container cranes. It looks like they will not surrender, and they are prepared to fight to the end," Alex said.

"Thank you. This is how we are going to proceed with the operation. The first thing that we are going to do is to roll out one armor vehicle in front of the truck so they can see it clearly. They will be requested to surrender through the vehicle's loudspeaker. The armed personnel in the vehicle will not step out at that moment. We will call them to surrender two times after those two times we would wait five minutes to see if there is any reaction to our request. Any questions at this point?" the General asked and looked at the members. "Let me continue. If the terrorists decide to surrender, then we order them to step out from the truck and lie down on the ground with their hands behind their heads. When they have done so, then the soldiers in the vehicle will step out and disarm them."

"What's our strategy if they open fire before we have ordered them to surrender?" one of the officers asked.

"We will, of course, return fire with the deadly force at once. There will be snipers placed at strategic positions at the port. Our personnel will have a clear view of the truck at all times."

General said and looked at Alex to see his reaction so far. "If they don't answer within those five minutes, then the armored vehicle will back off slowly from the truck. Then our strategy is to send one helicopter with soldiers to be dropped on top of the container roof. The mission here is to release the container from the truck if possible. The cargo in the container needs to be saved and confiscated undamaged. This action will also put more pressure on the suspects to surrender."

"This plan is on a very basic level without any details," the same officer said.

"We all know that there will be surprises. One of our strength in the Special Operation Force is the ability to improvise when things go another way, and we know it well," the General said with a big encouraging smile.

"What medical assistant do we have at the port?" another officer asked.

"We have the Army medical unit with full capability ready at close vicinity to the port. Two major hospitals have also been put on full emergency alert. I think that the suspects will not surrender, and they will be prepared to fight to their death. Let's get ready to execute the operation at first light tomorrow morning. If they decide to fight, we will give them a fight with only one outcome and that is elimination. Mr. Hen will be at the port too and he will travel in one of our armored vehicles with me. If you don't have more questions, then we shall rollout at five hundred hours tomorrow morning and take back the port. Good luck to you and your men," the General said looking at his watch.

The meeting was over, and all the officers that were ordered to take an active part in the operation, hurried back to their units to prepare for the operation. The General wanted to speak to Alex, so he stopped him before he left the conference room.

"Mr. Hen, I wanted to talk to you about one thing that concerns me. There are several international reporters with camera teams that have gathered around the port and around the port fence. Can you order the police force at the port to extend the security zone? You know that there can be heavy gunfire from the Army and the terrorists. Also, there can be other explosives involved based on what has happened to one of the cranes," the General said.

"I will send out the order for this right away," Alex said.

"Excellent, I trust you on this," the General said.

The General was to lead the operation from the armored vehicle by the army radio. Alex was to ride in the same armored vehicle with the General. This gave them the possibility to listen to all the operational orders and conversations of the whole operation.

□□□

The next morning several heavily armed Army vehicles were rolling through the port gate into the port. In one of the vehicles was the General and Alex sitting. This vehicle had specific flags to indicate that this was the General's staff vehicle. There was also the international press pushing to get access to the General, but they were kept at a distance by the police force. There was also a helicopter hovering at a distance. Local TV team was broadcasting live, close to the port gate. The Task Force team was now taking their positions on strategic places with a clear view of the truck. Everything was ready to execute the plan. The truck was in sight and the container was still attached to the truck.

Suddenly, the truck started to move slowly, and a voice was heard in the army's battle radio.

"Truck moving... truck moving. Regroup, regroup," the truck stopped closer to the sea than before but still was completely visible. The helicopter was now hovering closer to the truck but not taking any active part in the plan.

The General took the microphone in his armored vehicle and he was now giving orders to start the operation.

"Execute the plan. Roll out the vehicle in front of the truck," The General said. All teams were now in high alert and waiting for what was to happen when the men in the truck saw the armed vehicle rolling against them. The armed vehicle rolled slowly in front of the truck and stopped about fifty meters from the truck. The terrorists in the truck had now the full visibility to see the armored vehicle standing in front of them. Now, they were waiting but nothing happened. Only helicopter's sound could be heard at the port. Then a voice spoke from the armored vehicle's loudspeakers.

"This is the Army. You are surrounded by heavily armed military group. Surrender and come out from the truck with your hands above your heads. No one will be hurt if you surrender," the voice said, and this was the first request to surrender.

No reaction came from the truck and everything remained as calm and quiet as it was before while they waited for an answer. The terrorist could see that the snipers were regrouping to have a direct view of the truck cabin.

Again, a voice came from the armored vehicle that was stopped in front of the truck.

"This is the Army. You are surrounded by military force. Surrender and come out of the truck with your hands above your heads. No one will be hurt if you surrender," the voice said, and this was the second and last offer to the terrorists to surrender.

Suddenly the truck started to move against the armored vehicle. The truck stopped so close to the armored vehicle that they were now standing almost bumper to bumper. The General took the microphone.

"This is crazy. They really want to die in here. Back off from the truck, now... back off," he said, and the armored vehicle moved backward slowly until it reached a secure distance from the truck. Now the truck started to roll against the armored vehicle again, but this time much faster. The armored vehicle backed in between two containers and the opening was too narrow for the truck to follow so it stopped close to the gap. After a couple of minutes, the truck backed off from the narrow gap where the armored vehicle was.

"Helicopter action now. Board the container now," The General said in the radio.

The helicopter took the position right above the container. One of the Task Force soldiers started to glide down in the rope that was hanging down from the helicopter. He reached the container roof and lied flat down on the roof. Then the truck started to move forward and increasing speed so the helicopter above was also forced to increases its speeds to keep the position right above the container. There were two Task Force soldiers hanging on the rope under the helicopter and they were too high up to reach the container roof. The truck had now reached high speed and it was getting closer to a group of container cranes.

The helicopter pilot decided to abort the operation as it was already flying too close to the cranes. The pilot could not land so close to the cranes so the only possibility he had was to fly out above the sea with two soldiers hanging freely on the rope below. The helicopter was now flying over the sea with soldiers carrying heavy equipment in their backpacks. They couldn't hang too long under the helicopter. The General talked again into the microphone.

"Navy rescue... Navy rescue. Rescue boat needed outside the port. We have two men hanging under the helicopter, the General said on the radio.

The helicopter pilot spotted the Navy Rescue boat on the way to the port area. The pilot started to hover over the rescue boat and lower the helicopter so that the soldiers could enter the rescue boat safely. Both soldiers were now gliding down to the rescue boat and it all went well. The helicopter returned to circle at the port.

To avoid attacks from the air, the truck had now parked itself under one of the cranes. The plan to board the container from the air was now not an option if the truck stayed under the crane. One of the Task Force soldiers was lying on the container roof. The General communicated a clear order on the radio.

"Attention, attention. We have one of our soldiers lying on the container roof and he is alone. If people exited from the truck and try to climb up on the container roof, we will open fire on my command," the General said.

The armored vehicle with the General and Alex changed their position so they could see the back side of the container. The sniper team was also forced to change their tactical positions. The truck was now facing the sea, and this made the snipers possibility limited because they could not aim directly into the cabin.

After a couple of minutes, one of the truck's doors opened slowly without any person exiting the truck. After a couple of minutes an armed person slowly exited the truck. The person jumped down on the ground looking around and pointing his gun in all directions. At the same time, two of the snipers reported they have a clear lock on the target. Now everybody was waiting for the person from the truck to climb up and check the container roof. They could now see that the person was walking around the truck looking for something. When he reached the truck cabin he started to climb up to the container roof. The General was fast in the order.

"Hostile person outside the truck and climbing. Fire at will," he did not finish his sentence when loud gunshots were heard and then silence on the radio. Alex was getting worried about the silence.

"Why this silence and nothing reported? We clearly heard several guns fired," Alex said in a nervous voice.

"They wait if the terrorist on the ground is moving or not, or if there are other people coming out from the truck to help or climb up to the container roof. Let's wait and listen," the General whispered.

"Target outside the truck eliminated. No other people exiting the truck," the radios voice said.

The truck door opened again and an armed person exited the truck. The person was checking the surroundings and under the truck. He jumped into the truck again without checking further if the man on the ground was dead. The truck started to move forward slowly and they left the dead person lying on the ground.

"Truck moving... truck moving," the army radio cackled as one of the officers reported.

Everybody tried to understand in what direction the truck was heading. It was driving around in circles between the containers; the same route several times. Sometimes the opposite way than before, the whole thing was a mystery.

"Do they have communication with somebody outside the port and had requested help. That should not be possible because the whole mobile system was shut down. However, they could have some other options to communicate," the General said after minutes of silence and watching the truck driving around. "Hold your positions. Let's see what they are up to, now that the truck has stopped," the General said when the truck stopped between two containers.

Alex was sitting in the back of the armored vehicle without talking as much. He was nervous.

"I think they are getting desperate in the truck. They have no idea what to do and now one of their men is dead," the General said.

"What about the soldier on the container roof? Is he still lying there?" Alex asked.

"You are right, Mr. Hen, he is still there alone. I think he understands that he needs to find a better situation for himself. He is trained for it so I'm not worried. I have an idea about how we can get him out from there," the General said and grabbed the microphone to give a message.

"Attention, helicopter, make an attempt to rescue the soldier on the container roof," the General said.

"Roger."

The helicopter started to hover above the container with the rope hanging under it. The idea was that the helicopter will pass the truck at low speed and the soldier will grab the rope and be airlifted off the roof. This was a risky operation for the solider and the helicopter. Both were facing the possibility to be shot at when they fly away from the truck. They all understood that this must be done before any more offensive action was taken against the truck.

The helicopter approached the truck from behind to avoid getting shot at. Again, the truck started to roll forward. It was guessed that the men in the truck could hear the helicopter coming closer, so they decided to move around. The truck increased the speed to hide under the cranes but the helicopter caught up to the truck just before they reached the cranes. The solider on the container roof was standing up when he saw the helicopter coming at him with the rope hanging under. Now, the rope was above the container roof and the soldier jumped up to catch it. The helicopter needed to brake violently in midair to avoid a collision with the cranes and it was a close call but their work was done. The soldier was now hanging freely in the air under the helicopter and it turned to the sea to find the rescue boat. The General again gave the order via the radio.

"Navy rescue team, navy rescue team. Soldier hanging under the helicopter... activate a rescue mission."

The helicopter pilot saw the rescue boat at a distance and he turned to meet it. The soldier was sliding down to the rescue boat safely and was greeted by his colleagues in the rescue boat.

It was now late afternoon and the Task Force Soldiers had been in the port from early morning without food. The General was thinking of a plan on how to end the occupation without casualties before it gets dark. That was not an easy decision to make and if anything went wrong, he will be responsible for it.

However, he was responsible for the operation and only he could decide what the next step was, to end the occupation. When he was ready to communicate the next order the voice in the army radio said.

"Truck moving... truck moving and accelerating," radio voice said," it was from one of the officers.

All Task Force personnel were following the truck closely to understand where it was going. The truck was now moving with very high speed between the containers. The General's armored vehicle and the other vehicles had to change their positions to see where the truck was going. The only thing they could see was a cloud of dust where the truck was. In the army radio, there was somebody screaming.

"It's going for the gate. The truck is going for the gate at high speed."

The voice screamed.

The General and Alex understood that the truck was going to force it through the guarded gate. This was a dangerous situation for the personnel guarding the gate. They must be warned. The General grabbed his army microphone and Alex his police radio microphone and they both were now screaming orders to their personnel.

"Fire at will... fire at will... Stop the truck from reaching the gate," the General screamed.

"All units at the gate...all gate units. Exit your vehicles... exit your vehicles now. The Truck is going to ram the gate at high speed," Alex screamed.

The heavy gunfire could now be heard from several locations at the port. All soldiers on the ground and snipers who could aim at the truck were now firing with all they had but the truck was still rolling in a cloud of dust. The Port Master who stood at the port office window could now see the police exiting the cars and running from the gate. The riot wagon backed off from the gate but there were still some trucks parked in front of the gates with no drivers inside. There was no sign that the truck will slow down or stop before the gate. They realized that they could not stop the truck as it was now going to reach the gate with high speed.

The truck reached the gate with a crash sound and then an enormous explosion followed. The whole truck cabin was blown away by an explosion. The gate flew at the port's office wall and the trailer with the container was lifted backward a couple of meters and then rolled back until it hit other containers. The windows at the Port Master's office were blown inside because of the blast. Everything was now covered in smoke and dust. The truck had managed to break through the line of police cars and trucks that were blocking the gate. Several of the police cars were lying upside down and burning. Everything looked like a war zone. Shortly after the explosion the General and Alex reached the gate with their armored vehicle. They both stepped out from the vehicle watching speechless at the disaster. The policemen that had left the cars at the gate were now walking back to the gate and brushing off the dust from their uniforms. They recognized that Alex was standing by the burning police cars, so they walked to him.

"That was a close call, I must say," one of the policemen said standing beside Alex.

"Yes, it was close. Have you counted all men here?" Alex asked.

"All are okay, but our cars have some damage. The damage report will be complicated to write when we return to the office," one officer said pointing to several police cars that were burning and lying upside down. They all smiled at the statement and they were happy that all police officers were unhurt.

The General was walking around in the debris looking for something. Alex was interested in what he was looking for.

"General, what are you looking for in the debris maybe we can help?" Alex asked.

"I'm looking for the terrorist's weapons. Their weapon should remain intact even after the explosion. We must find them as those might give us important information about weapons' origin and type. Based on this information we might be able to understand where the terrorists were coming from or who supported them with weapons," the General said.

"Excuse me, General, but that is the work for our forensic team. I guess they are on the way here right now," Alex said.

"You are right. I'm sorry; it's an old habit to jump into a war zone. This needs to be handled in the civil world," the General said smiling.

They could now see the fire department and the ambulances coming to the port. It was impossible to drive into the port due to all the debris that was burning and lying in front of the gate. The fire department started to put out the fire by spraying extinguishers on all burning cars. The first ambulance was helping people injured due to flying debris when they walked on the street pavement close to the gate.

Another ambulance stopped and helped a biker that was sitting on the pavement shocked and confused. Fire rescue truck was checking the port office and found the Port Master lying on the floor injured from the flying glass when the window was blown inside of the explosion. The police stopped all traffic on the Keppler Road. This road was passing close to the gate and there was debris lying on the whole road blocking it.

The General walked back to the armored vehicle to send out an order to the Task Force. The Task Force was still holding their positions inside the port as ordered. They were ordered to do so until a new order was given. The General took the microphone and gave the order.

"All Army and Navy officers at the port. Count your men and equipment. Report to me when done," the General said.

After a couple of minutes, all officers reported that all the soldiers were accounted for and no material was missing. The General was very pleased with the result. He had promised at the briefing that there would not be any casualties apart from the terrorists eliminated if needed and the port occupation stopped. For him, this was a success and a result of their tactical planning that his officers had developed and executed. Alex turned to the General to ask him what really happened.

"General, what happened here? Did you do anything?" Alex asked.

"No, we didn't do anything. We only opened fire when the truck was driving full speed against the gate."

"It was a suicide decision on their side instead of surrendering. I think it's the same type of fanatic ideology in play when we see this done by the suicide bombers. Here, it was the whole group's decision," the General said.

"That is possible, but it could also be the case that the bomb exploded by mistake inside the truck. Maybe they were in the process of preparing the bomb when it exploded in the truck instead of the intended targeted place. This is, of course, speculation and nothing can be proved," Alex said.

Alex was now much more concerned about the complexity of the container case, after the explosion. He started to worry about the possibility that he could not solve the case at all. He decided to call the Commissioner. The Commissioner answered directly and started to speak before Alex could explain what had happened.

"Yes, Alex. I saw it on the news it's everywhere now; here and also internationally. Any injuries or worse?"

"No, all men are okay, but we have severe material damages and we lost a number of police vehicles. Let's talk more tomorrow. I need to talk to my men now," Alex said.

The news media was now reporting live from the port and they wanted to get some comments from Alex. But he was prepared with one and only standard issued answer for now.

"Investigation is still ongoing, and we will come back to you when we have more to report, " Alex said.

"It's been a long day," the General said.

"Yes, I think that we are going to be really busy tomorrow," Alex said and jumped into a civil police car and the General was picked up by an army vehicle.

———◆———

PART SIX

The Conclusion

Chapter

13

Alex arrived early to the office this morning after a night without any sleep. He had been thinking the whole night about the case and finally came to an insight that he must establish a scenario with all the information available. The only thing the investigators had at this point was a lot of information but no scenarios on how all the facts were connected and ended with the terrible explosion at the port. He walked into the coffee room for coffee and decided to turn on the TV.

The morning news had already started with a live broadcast from local and international TV teams. Alex could see on the TV that the forensic team was already at the port to collect all the pieces from the explosion. Several police officers were walking in the debris to pick up small fragments of interest and placing sticks with white flags where human remains were found. The Army's bomb squad team was also in the port to screen the area for any possible explosive material remaining in the port. The whole port was now sealed off as a crime scene.

Ajay arrived at the office and he walked directly into the coffee room.

"Good morning, Ajay. Have you watched the morning news?" Alex asked.

"No, I have been listening to the news on the radio in my car," Ajay said

"Several international TV teams are broadcasting live from the port. I switched on the TV to see if our Police Commissioner has stepped forward to give any comments," Alex said.

"What I know is that we have nothing to say to the press for now," Ajay said.

"You are right we have nothing to say and that is the problem. What we need to do now is to build a scenario of the case with all the pieces we have. I think we start with your part of the investigation with the dead bodies," Alex said.

Alex and Ajay walked to the conference room and Ajay started to note his findings on the whiteboard.

"I will only write short facts of our findings," Ajay said when he picked up a whiteboard pen and Alex nodded to agree.

Ajay started by dividing the whiteboard into two parts to indicate the two dead bodies. Ajay wrote on one side of the whiteboard.

Bedok Reservoir, unidentified man, the tattoo with characters on the left upper arm, one photo, no address, frequent travel to Singapore, connected to the Russian weapons dealer, dead before dumped into the water, murdered by poisoning, no witness and no other clues.

Ajay sat down at the back of the conference room watching the whiteboard with all the facts he had just written.

"You see that we don't have many facts about this man's death," Alex said standing up and started to walk around in the room.

Ajay could see that Alex was worried about the fact that there was nothing to report. Ajay walked to the whiteboard and continued to write on the other half.

Bedok Town Park, Russian man, weapons dealer, internationally known, shot at close range, park workers clothes found, the tattoo with characters on the left upper arm and the photo found in the dead man's shoe at the reservoir.

"That is it. That's all we have, and I must admit that it's not much either. We have done all the right things in our investigations. Taken in all the possibilities we had," Ajay said looking at the whiteboard from a distance.

Alex could see that Ajay was not happy about the result either, so Alex decided to give Ajay some positive feedback.

"Ajay, I know you are disappointed with your results and I'm also disappointed. However, sometimes an investigator must face the facts that there are no more clues even if you try hard to find them. This goes with the profession. Like a football player who is the best in the world, but in one of his games, he misses a penalty kick. However, he is still considered to be one of the best in the world. The player accepts this because it belongs to his profession."

"Alex, I understand your point and that was a good explanation. I will start to think like that and thanks for your understanding."

Hamid walked into the conference room and started to study the words on the whiteboard. Ajay and Alex waited for his comments, but he was silent. Hamid took the pen and drew a new line to divide the whiteboard to add a new section of facts.

"I have done some investigation of the truck and I want to show it to you here and now," Hamid said and started to write on the whiteboard.

Stolen truck from Malaysia, stolen Singapore number plates, false documents to access the port area, Suicide bomb or mistake caused of the explosion and persons in the truck are unidentified.

"Hamid, well done, you have added some new information that we did not know before," Alex said and put his hand over Hamid's shoulder to show that he cares about him.

Amanda walked into the conference room with a smile in her face and singing. The others in the room were waiting for the information that had made her so happy.

"They have called from the hospital that Kevin has recovered well, and he will be okay. The good news was that we can visit him now," Amanda said with a smile on her face.

"Let's go there and buy some flowers for him," Alex said and they all rushed out of the conference room to visit Kevin.

They arrived at the hospital where Kevin was being treated for his gunshot wound. He was lying in his bed half asleep when Alex, Amanda, Ajay, and Hamid walked into his room.

"Hi, young man, good to see you alive. I'm hoping to see you at the office soon because we need your help," Alex said with a smile and showed Kevin the flowers.

Kevin was smiling mildly to avoid pain in his wound. He could not sit upright but he could talk slowly. "Well, young is an overestimation but I'm happy to see you all here. I hope someone is answering to incoming calls at the office when you are here, Amanda," Kevin said and touching his wound with his hand.

"Don't talk if you have pain. We are happy to see your old face without talking," Hamid said, and Kevin started laughing with a painful expression on his face.

"Do you know what has happened?" Alex asked.

Kevin nodded and pointed towards the TV in the room. They could see that he had a remote control to operate the TV.

"I was lucky that it was a small caliber handgun and nothing else. I should have listened to you, Hamid. I had been wondering over one thing since I woke up, was it our container that the truck was pulling?" Kevin asked and looked at Hamid.

"Yes, it was our container. They picked it up the same day as the crane would have loaded it on the vessel. They probably knew exactly what day and time the loading was planned to occur. It was easy to grab it on the loading day without any suspicions. They have also used false papers to get access to the port and the truck that was stolen from Malaysia. It was a perfect plan," Hamid said.

"Lucky that you had the number printed on your brain and caught it as soon as you saw it," Kevin spoke in a low voice.

"We were lucky to spot the truck at the right time. If we haven't been walking at the port area nobody would have noticed that the container was transported out from the port," Hamid said.

"You both did a good job in transporting the container from the hangar to the port, but the rest of the operation was a disaster," Alex said and they all laughed to the boss's feedback.

"What about the explosion that blew away the truck cabin. Was it an Army's decision?" Kevin asked.

"No, actually we don't know why it happened and I guess we will never know exactly why it happened. It could have been their intention for a planned suicide explosion or a mistake when they were preparing the bomb inside the truck. I was there at the port when it happened. I was sitting in one of the army's armored vehicles with the General himself and he had no clue either," Alex said.

"Good that you also had the possibility to see some action in the field," Kevin said, and they were all laughing again.

One of the hospital nurses walked into the room and said that the visiting time was over as Kevin still needed to rest. They all walked out of the door but waved to Kevin first and he waved slowly with the hand above the gunshot wound.

"See you soon at the office, Kevin," Hamid said and closed the door.

They were all sitting silently in the car when they traveled back to the office. When they arrived, they walked into the conference room to continue their conclusion writing on the whiteboard.

"Hamid, your information that the truck was stolen and had false registration plates is interesting," Alex said and took a whiteboard pen to draw a new vertical line. He wrote the heading.

Persons in the truck.

He stood there thinking before writing, but he could only write one single fact.

Four persons inside the truck.

"I feel that we don't have a lot of facts about the persons in the truck, only that they were four people," Alex said and laid down the pen.

Hamid took the pen and wrote under his column.

Persons in the truck still not identified. The truck was stolen in Malaysia. Stolen registration plates in Singapore. Who stole the truck? Who stole the registration plates?

"This tells me that we need to find the facts in those areas with question marks. Hamid, can you make contact with the forensic team and investigate what they have found?" Alex said and Hamid nodded. He walked back to his desk.

Alex began to understand that keeping Ajay focused on the two dead men was not going to bring the case any forward. He decided to give him another task to focus on.

"Ajay, I want you to contact the Malaysian Police and check with them what they have about the stolen truck. You know dates, times witness, etc. and with the Singapore, Police to know about the stolen registration plates. What do you think about that"? Alex asked Ajay.

"That is fine with me and I can start right now," Ajay said and walked out of the conference room.

Hamid started to search in the forensic database if the forensic team had added anything new from the port. He found some new photos and one specific photo of a partly burned backpack caught his eyes. He decided to go down to the forensic department and talk to them.

□□□

After a couple of hours, Alex's mobile rang and he could see that it was Hamid calling, so he answered.

"Alex, here. That is interesting. Yes, we will start to investigate that right away. Great job, Hamid," Alex said and hung up.

"Ajay. It was Hamid calling from the forensic team. They have found a fragment of a hotel bill in the backpack that was half burned. It's a Hotel located in the Katong area," Alex said.

"Great, we need to investigate that at once. I will take Hamid with me," Ajay said and walked down to the forensic department to pick up Hamid.

Ajay and Hamid were on the way to the port to study the piece of paper more closely. When they arrived, they walked to the forensic wagon where all the debris of interest was collected. One of the forensic police was guarding the forensic wagon.

"Morning. I'm Ajay and this is Hamid and here are our badges. We work at the Criminal Investigations Department. We want to have access to all your findings here at the port. We don't need to take anything with us only to review it for further investigations," Ajay said.

The forensic police checked their badges carefully and opened the door to the specially equipped forensic truck as they all stepped inside. There were a lot of plastic bags on the shelves with debris collected. There was also a freezer to store human remains however they were not interested in that material this time.

"We are specifically interested in the piece of paper where a Hotel in Katong could be identified?" Ajay asked the forensic police in the wagon.

"I understand. I called your office to inform you about it. Here it is in this plastic bag. It's not a big piece but you can read it in the half-burned area," the forensic police said and gave Ajay the plastic bag without taking it from the plastic bag. The piece of paper must remain inside the plastic bag to avoid contamination. Ajay was looking closely at the paper inside the plastic bag, but he couldn't read it. He gave the plastic bag to Hamid, so he so can look at it.

"I can't read it. It's impossible," Hamid said and gave the plastic bag back to the forensic police.

"Sorry, I forgot that you have to look at it with a specific electronic magnifier," the forensic police said and gave Hamid some type of glasses that he could put on.

"Wow, now I can see the text clearly. Yes, it's a hotel but it's not possible to see the complete name. The whole address can't be read. I can read Katong but not the whole address. Hope that there aren't so many hotels on that street," Hamid said and gave the electronic glasses to Ajay, so he also can look at it.

"Fantastic. I can see it now. Hamid, take a pen and write down my comments as I tell them," Ajay said, and Hamid picked up his pen and a notebook.

"Okay. Hamid, I will start to read it for you. Information collected from the piece of half burned paper at the forensic wagon located at the port. The text hotel can be seen together with part of the address Marina Parade and Katong. Nothing more can be read from the paper fragment." Ajay said and took off his electronic glasses.

"I have it all written here. Do I have to write a report about this?" Hamid asked and showed Ajay his notes.

"No, only later when we have more we can write a report. So let's start to check all hotels in Katong and the Marina Parade," Ajay said and walked out from the forensic wagon and Hamid walked after him.

Both men were now sitting silently in the police car without saying anything. They were both thinking deeply about what the next step should be in the investigation.

"Hamid, do you have an idea, what action we should take to continue the investigation?" Ajay asked.

"Huh..? Yeah. The next important step for me would be to visit Kevin and inform him about our finding," Hamid said looking deeply into Ajay's eyes to emphasize that he was serious about it.

"Really? Do you mean that?" Ajay asked in a surprised voice.

"I'm serious, Ajay, and I want to go there right away."

Ajay did not say anything but he started the engine, looked at his watch and started to roll. Hamid noted that they were on the way to the hospital to visit Kevin. Ajay knew that Criminal Investigators on duty missions didn't need to follow the strict and limited visitors' time. They arrived at the hospital and passed the reception area smoothly after showing their badges. They could not carry flowers since they were on an investigation mission. They stopped outside Kevin's room when they saw that his lunch meal was carried out from his room.

"He is recovering well. I can see that Kevin has eaten all his food, the plate is empty," Ajay said and they both entered Kevin's room laughing.

"Kevin, you old man. You are recovering nicely," Ajay said with a smile.

"You are a good investigator. I guess you checked my tray to get this correct conclusion," Kevin said, and they were all laughing again.

This time Kevin was also laughing without any indication of too much pain in his chest.

"Nice of you to visit me; an inactive investigator checked in here at this hospital. I guess you must be busy with your case and now with the explosion at the port. Who knows where this is going?" Kevin said.

"The hacker is doing fine. He has some notes from the port. We drove here directly from the forensic team at the port," Ajay said and tapped Hamid on his shoulder.

"So, Hamid, tell me what you have from the forensic team?" Kevin asked and looked at Hamid.

"We have only a little piece of a half-burnt paper with the words hotel in Katong and partly the address at Marina

Parade. This is the only thing that we could read from the paper and nothing more," Hamid said.

"Hmm... I have had a similar case a long time ago. We did not have the name of the person or hotel only small partly readable address to work on."

Ajay and Hamid were interested to listen to Kevin's experience from a similar situation. Kevin continued to talk when he saw that both Ajay and Hamid were interested in his story.

"We forced all hotels in the area to contact the Criminal Department and report every case they had when people did not check out in time. We waited a couple of days and finally, one hotel contacted us. We checked the hotel room together with the forensic team and found all the evidence we needed to take the case to prosecution and the guilty were convicted," Kevin said.

Ajay and Hamid looked at each other with their mouths open. They realized that Kevin had just given them exactly the advice they needed to proceed with the case. Even Ajay must recognize Kevin's advice.

"Kevin, thank you, that you share your experience with a similar case. Now we know how to proceed and that is because of your experience," Ajay said.

"Don't let me delay you in your investigation. Go out there and execute according to my advice and thank you again for the visit," Kevin said and waved to Ajay and Hamid to leave the room.

Ajay and Hamid left Kevin's room in a hurry. They were now on the way back to the office and start the hotel investigation exactly the way as Kevin had told them. Ajay and Hamid walked directly into Alex's office when they arrived. They talked about forensic finding and advice from Kevin. The focus was now to find the right hotel and secure any information related to that.

"Gentlemen, well done both of you. I will call for an information meeting first thing tomorrow and put all the men in the office to work on this," Alex said and stood up to indicate that the meeting was over. Alex and Hamid left the office.

Alex walked to Amanda to call for the information meeting next morning.

"Amanda, we need to have all investigators in the conference room tomorrow morning for an information meeting," Alex said.

"Tomorrow morning. You know it's already late in the day and this is a short notice. It can be hard to reach all the investigators before tomorrow morning," Amanda said.

"Everybody needs to be there and it's mandatory," Alex said.

"What is the agenda for this meeting? It has to be a good agenda for a meeting at such short notice," Amanda said.

"How would this agenda be received... the 'salary increase discussion for this year and priority," Alex said and they both started laughing.

Amanda understood the sarcastic comment, but it also meant that Amanda must create a good agenda as the topic when she called everyone to the meeting.

Ajay and Hamid were watching TV news in the coffee room. It was a live broadcast and they could see that almost all debris from the explosion was removed. The port's office's crashed windows were now covered with wooden boards. They had both just received the mandatory call to a morning meeting tomorrow. Amanda's creative agenda topic was, 'Redistribution of responsibilities at the department'.

———◆———

Chapter

14

The morning meeting was well attended by all the investigators and they were now gathered in the conference room. Alex entered the room and started to talk.

"Welcome, all. First, I want to report the good news about Kevin. He is recovering well, and he is expected to be working in the office from the next week. Second, is that we have a new clue to work one and that is a piece of paper found in the port indicating a hotel located in the Katong area somewhere at Marina Parade. We don't know exactly the hotel name and we know there are several hotels on that street. We need to visit all of them and give them the instructions that they must report to us directly if they have any guest that has not checked out in time. We need to start this right now from today. Any questions so far?" Alex asked. No questions were coming from the staff but some head shaking as other ongoing investigations were stopped for the time being. Alex continued. "Hamid will be responsible to provide a list of all hotels and the addresses. Ajay issued one hotel to each man. This person will also act as a single point of contact when the hotel has something to report. Any questions about this?" Alex asked.

"What is the status of the two dead men related to this case?" one investigator asked.

Ajay stood up and started to answer the question, but Alex stopped him by indicating that he should sit down. Alex started to answer instead.

"The investigation about the two dead men is now temporarily on hold because we have no trace to work on. That case as a whole is, of course, related to the port explosion. Now let's go out there and find something that will crack this case. We need that," Alex said.

The meeting was over and all the staff left the conference room. Amanda walked to Hamid's desk as he was deeply involved in something that he had ongoing on his displays.

"I heard that you visited Kevin. Did he miss work?" Amanda asked.

"He was in his most positive mood and interested to hear about our case. It was his idea to proceed with the hotel investigation that Alex talked about," Hamid said.

"It's nice to hear that he is in a positive mode and recovering well," Amanda said and walked to her desk.

Hamid started studying the information on his display where he had searched for all hotels at the Marina Parade. He was a little bit stressed since all investigators were now waiting for his information before they could start the work together with Ajay.

He printed out all hotels' names with the addresses and delivered them to Ajay. It was his duty to assign the hotels to individual investigators. All investigators had departed to hotels at the Marina Parade. Everything was now quite at the office. Hamid was looking out from the office and he felt a little bit disappointed that he did not get any assignment.

Alex was in his office reading some documents when his phone rang. There was nothing on the display to show who was calling. He hesitated to answer for a while but then he answered. The caller was a newly hired young investigator and he was on his first field mission.

"Yes, Alex here. Hi. Have we met? I understand so you are new to our department. You say that you are at the hotel in Katong and there is something of interest in the hotel you are in right now. There is a guest who has first extended the stay in the hotel and not checked out as planned. Correct? Now the sign 'Do not disturb' is hanging outside the hotel room door," Alex said and started to walk around in the office while listening.

"What is the hotel guest's name? Are you kidding me is it really the Nikolaj Puchkov? Is this possible? It's the name of the man we found dead at the Bedok City Park the Russian weapons dealer. Ask for permission to enter the hotel room; it's an emergency. I will be on my way and don't touch anything," Alex said.

He passed Amanda's desk to inform her where he was going and the reason. Amanda waved to him that she got the message.

Alex arrived at the hotel and the front desk sent him to the third floor in room number 314. The investigator that had called Alex was there outside the door together with the hotel's security Manager. The hotel security Manager opened the door slowly and the investigator entered first with his gun drawn. He checked the toilet and the wardrobes before Alex and the hotel security guard could enter.

There were several empty pizza boxes and beer cans laying around together with hamburger boxes. With his experience from field work he directly could evaluate that the room has been occupied by several people for several days. There was also a half open bag on the floor containing something that looked like ammunition in different calibers. The investigator called the forensic office and requested a team to be sent to the hotel. Two forensic investigators arrived within ten minutes and started their work inside the Hotel room. Alex and the investigator could walk around in the room without touching anything.

One of the forensic people wanted Alex to come to the toilet and Alex walked in there.

"Alex. Look, this small bag containing needles in a plastic box," the forensic guy said.

"Don't open it. I think it contains some type of Russian poison from world war two," Alex said holding up his hand.

The other forensic investigator found two passports and credit cards in a plastic bag. He wanted Alex and the investigator to look at them. The investigator could not tell anything about the passports, however, Alex recognized both men.

"This passport belongs to the man we found dead at the Bedok Reservoir. His passport is South Korean but it's a fake. The other passport belongs to a Russian man that was found dead in Bedok City Park," Alex said.

"The names on the credit cards match the name on the passports. They have been taken in connection to the murder I guess," the investigator said and gave all the credit cards and passports to the forensic people.

They also found several pistols and one of them was equipped with a muffler. Alex asked the forensic guy to check the pistol with the muffler mounted on it. He wanted to know if it had been used recently.

"I can see that it has been used. There are several indicators that point to that direction. One thing is that the cartridge case is partly filled and the recognizable smell of burned gunpowder," forensic investigator said and turned the pistol around in his plastic covered hands.

"Fantastic. I think this is the pistol that was used to murder the Russian man," Alex said and walked to the other investigator.

"Can you call Ajay; I guess you know him? Tell him that I want him here at the hotel now. I want him to coordinate all the interesting facts found in this room and to consolidate the results from the interviews we got from the hotel personnel. He has to report the result at my office today before he goes home. I will wait for his report," Alex said to the investigator.

"Yes, sir, I know Ajay. I will call him straight away," the investigator said and walked outside the hotel room to call him.

The forensic team was ready with the crime scene investigation and they were now collecting all the findings into plastic bags for further laboratory analysis. As they completed, they all started to leave the room. Alex drove back to the office and the investigator started to call in more investigators to the hotel to have a fast result from the interviews. All hotel staff were now about to be questioned for information on the guests' activities.

Alex arrived at the office with a smile on his face. Hamid was at the office looking up over his wall of displays and Amanda walked after Alex into his office.

"I see a smile on your face, I guess that we have something to work on from the hotel you have visited?" Amanda asked.

"The hotel will provide us with a good piece of evidence how the men were murdered. Our first theory was correct however, we don't know who murdered them and why," Alex said.

"Good day for you today then. Nice to hear that we are moving forward after several days of having nothing to work on," Amanda said and started to walk out of Alex's office, but Alex stopped her.

"Can you request Hamid to come into my office?". Amanda nodded.

☐☐☐

Amanda walked to Hamid and asked him to go to Alex's office. She also grabbed the opportunity to joke with him about the reason he has been called to Alex office.

"Hamid, Alex wants you to come to his office at once. He is upset about something that you have been involved in," Amanda said.

Hamid jumped up behind his displays, his face was totally white.

"What can it be? I don't know what mistake I have done," Hamid said and started to walk to Alex's office. He knocked on the door before entering.

"Hamid, good that you are here. I have a task for you that is important." Alex said and collected the documents that were lying on his desk and gave them to Hamid.

Hamid took the pack of documents in his hand and watched Alex at the same time with a surprised look on his face. He was waiting for some hard criticism over something that he was involved in but nothing of that type came from Alex.

"What shall I do with this pack of papers?" Hamid asked.

"You shall build a presentation of the whole case that we have worked on. You take all the notes from the documents you are holding in your hand. All notes we have written on the whiteboard and all information from the forensic department related to the findings both in the port and at the hotel are in there," Alex said with a smile.

"Hotel, what hotel? Have we found something to work on?"

"Hamid, we have found evidence that can verify our theory how the two men were murdered however, we don't know by who and why."

"This is news to me. I haven't heard anything from the hotel investigators."

"Of course, not. It happened just an hour ago, Hamid," Alex said with a huge laugh that could be heard in the whole office, and a raised eye. He also waved in the direction of the door to indicate that Hamid could now leave his office and start with the assignment.

Hamid walked by Amanda's desk and she was laughing but wasn't saying anything. Hamid had now an important part of the investigation and that was to recreate the total scenario of the case with all strange events. He took the documents and walked to his desk shaking his head at Amanda. He realized he was 'pranked' on. He felt relieved that he was not in trouble for anything. Instead, he felt a little stressed over the new assignment that he had received from Alex.

At the same time, Ajay arrived back from the hotel investigation and he walked directly to Alex's office. He knocked on the door and Alex waved to him that it was okay to enter.

"Ajay, what have you found from the hotel staff?" Alex asked.

Ajay opened his notebook and started telling about the interview results. "The hotel room was booked in the name of Nikolaj Puchkov, the same man that was found murdered at the Bedok City Park. His credit card was used for the payment. He extended his stay at the hotel by three days. This request was done from his room phone. Note that Nikolaj Puchkov had been already found dead when the additional stay for three days was requested," Ajay said.

"How could they extend the stay for an additional three days without asking for ID's or something?" Alex asked.

"The front desk can verify the correct room number by the phone number the call was coming from. All internal hotel calls with room numbers are displayed at the front desk. The front desk extended the stay for three days and his credit card was used to cover the extension cost," Ajay said.

"Okay, so that is how it worked. It was a smart move to finance the extension and grab the room without showing who they really were," Alex said.

"The interesting thing is that from the extension day onwards, the sign of 'do not disturb' has been hanging outside the hotel room. The result of this is that no cleaning service had been possible these days. The guest had been eating breakfast every morning in the first period at the stay, but he was never eating breakfast within the extension days," Ajay said.

"I have a feeling that these terrorists knew what they were doing. Scary in a way for us," Alex said.

"My conclusion is that somebody related to the terrorists or one of them called from the Russian man's room and requested an extension of the stay. When this was done they all could use the hotel room through the hotel garage elevator. They could use the hotel room key to operate the elevator to the floor where the room was. Based on the number of food supply cartons that were found, we can see that they were four persons eating in the room for at least two days," Ajay said.

"What triggered the hotel to reveal this to our investigators? They have the credit card and they had approved the extension. So, nothing really prevented them to be suspicious," Alex asked.

"When one of our investigators arrive at the hotel, they told him that the guest first has extended the stay and then not checked out in time. Then the hotel security Manager and our investigator called you about it," Ajay said.

"The Russian man was not murdered and robbed for the purpose to use his credit cards, money, and the passport to secure a hotel room under a false name. What do you think, Ajay?" Alex asked.

"No way. That can't be the only reason. It was part of their smart and creative plan. The Russian man killed the man that was found in Bedok Park and then the Russian man was killed by the terrorists to take the container. It has been established by Interpol that he was an international arms smuggler. So we can't deviate from that. We can say, it was a smart and creative plan and we spoiled it for them," Ajay said.

"You are right. Well done. You should now write a complete report and give it to Hamid. He is working on a presentation package," Alex said.

❑❑❑

Hamid had been at the forensic department to investigate if they had found anything more from the material they collected at the hotel. When he entered the office, Alex waved to him to come. Hamid walked to Alex's office.

"Hamid, anything new from the forensic department?" Alex asked.

"Yes, indeed. They have found our container ID written

on a page in the hotel room's notebook. You know those which are just lying around in all the hotel rooms. It was the correct and complete container ID. The number of our container together with a phone number starting with the Russian country code. The forensic team called the number, but the subscriber could not be reached," Hamid said.

"There is another connection to the Russian man and our container. They removed the mobile phone from the Russian man when he was left dead in the park," Ajay said.

"With this new material, we definitely have something to communicate to the Police Commissioner and inform her about what we have," Alex said and walked to Amanda to set up a meeting with the Commissioner.

———◆———

PART SEVEN

The Reporting

Chapter

15

Alex was now on the way to meet the Commissioner and he was in a very good mood this time. He knew that he had a lot to report and several leads to work on. He hoped that the Commissioner would be pleased with the progress.

Alex knew the procedure that the Commissioner's secretary used. When Alex entered the office, he sat down on the sofa in front of the secretary and waited for the sign. The secretary gave him an elegant hand signal with her long perfect painted nails when he could enter the Commissioner's office. No words were needed everything was effective and smooth.

Inside, he sat down in one of the leather chairs in front of her desk.

"Welcome, Alex. It's good that you have something to report. Time is flying, and a lot of things have happened. Tell me about it," Catherine said.

Alex reported all the findings of the case including the latest information received from the hotel. He also mentioned the complete presentation that Hamid was working on. The presentation will be presented to the Commissioner's Committee when all facts would be on the table. Lastly, of course, the news that Kevin was recovering well from the gunshot. Alex took a break in his reporting and kept looking at the Commissioner for a while to understand if she had any questions so far.

"Your report is very good, and I'm pleased with the progress. I understand that you have some concerns and unclear areas you want to talk about. Can you report to me more about those areas, maybe I can help in some way?" Catherine asked.

"Of course. I'm disappointed that we don't have all the needed answers today, but we are working hard to solve the remaining question marks. Let me continue," Alex said and picked up his notebook in which he had made notes related to the unsolved areas. He started to explain that to Catherine.

"There are two major things that I can't understand or report clearly. The first one is that we don't know the reason why the container ID number was tattooed on the upper left arm and for what purpose? The second is more difficult and of most concern to me. What are the terrorists' agenda and goal? What was their nationality... we don't know. We don't know when they entered the country… We don't know what support they have locally... We don't know if there are terrorist cells in our country to be activated when needed? One of the issues is also, of course, where are they getting the financial support? Weapon, ammunition and logistics support does not come for free. It costs a lot," Alex said and laid down his notebook on Catherine's desk.

He had now reported everything both in success and what was remaining. He felt relieved to have told everything they investigated. He was now looking at Catherine to understand how she'd comment on the unsolved and unexplained areas of the case.

"Alex, you guys have done well in the investigation. Let's see what I can do to help you. I can't promise anything, but my international contacts can give us some pieces in the missing puzzle," Catherine said and stood up to indicate that the meeting was over.

Alex left the conference room relaxed and convinced that Catherine will pull some international strings to get help. The whole case had an international dimension.

Alex returned to the office where all was quite as usual. Hamid was working with high dedication in finalizing the reports with all the pieces that he needed to collect. Ajay was writing on his hotel interview report for Hamid and Amanda was trying to finalize the damage report for all the police cars that were destroyed at the port. Insurance reporting and the Criminal Investigation Departments activities were not an easy combination to explain to the insurance companies.

Suddenly, Amanda rushed into Alex's office with a paper in her hand. Hamid could see that Amanda and Alex were discussing intensely. After a while, Amanda walked to the coffee room and Alex rushed out of the office. Hamid was interested in what was going on, so he walked to the coffee room to find out from Amanda if she would say something.

"It is always this quite in the office when everybody has gone for field work," Hamid said and pressed some buttons for coffee.

"Yes. And now Alex also must leave the office in a hurry. He was called to an urgent meeting with the Police Commissioner. They wanted Alex to be at the meeting at once."

"Urgent... what was it about? He was almost running. I have never seen him rush out from the office like that."

"Maybe I should not say this, but it was about the tattoos on the dead men."

"Are you sure? This is strange that the Police Commissioner suddenly wanted to talk about the dead men and their tattoos."

"We have nothing new to report. The only thing we can report is that we have nothing more to report. That was also Alex's opinion that it's a waste of time to meet the Commissioner right now. Finally, he decided to meet the Commissioner and that was the reason for the rush. I guess he was upset about the fact that he did not have anything to report."

☐☐☐

Alex entered the Commissioner's office. The secretary was waiting for him and waved to Alex that he can enter the Commissioner's office without sitting and waiting. He entered her office with a light knock on the door before opening it.

Alex noticed that the Commissioner was not alone in the office. There was also a man wearing a dark suit with a brown suitcase on the desk in front of him. He was expecting the man to leave the Commissioner's office when he entered, but that did not happen. Instead, Catherine showed with her hand that Alex should sit down.

"Alex, thank you for coming on such short notice. May I introduce to you to Mr. Steven Newbridge from one of our allied embassies and this is Mr. Alex Hen. He is the Head of our Criminal Investigation Department," Catherine said, and both men shook hands.

Alex did not know the man in the room. What organization was this man representing? Can it be MI5, CIA or other agent organizations in the Asia region? The man's language and dialect sounded both American and British at the same time and this was confusing. The expression that Catherine was using was our 'allied countries'. This meant that she didn't want to reveal the country by name. Alex was used to it, so he did not ask about it.

"Mr. Newbridge has some information about the tattoos. However, he will not reveal that here and now because under normal circumstances he should not know these facts at all. He is here to help us with the investigation. Mr. Newbridge, can you explain further?" Catherine asked.

"Thank you, Commissioner. I have arranged a meeting with a man that the Commissioner and I trust fully and he will tell you everything about those tattoos. The meeting is arranged tomorrow at 3pm at the East Coast Park and it's at the place called Marin Cove. You must be there tomorrow on time and he will tell you all about it," Mr. Newbridge said.

"That would be a great help for us. How can I identify the man at the Marin Cove and where? There are several restaurants in that place," Alex said.

"You order a cup of coffee and you select a table placed at the short end of the building facing the sea. You will not recognize the person you are going to meet instead he will recognize you," Mr. Newbridge said with a smile.

Alex made some notes about the meeting place and time. He also wrote down some questions that he was planning to ask Mr. Newbridge.

"Alex, you shall also write down all the information what this man will tell you. Your notes will be part of the official Government report and it will be classified as a top secret when it's written. The man you are going to meet there has our full trust. Any questions Alex?" Catherine asked.

Mr. Newbridge was nodding to confirm what Catherine was saying.

"Can I take some of my investigators with me to this meeting?" Alex asked.

"Sorry, sir, but this is a one-man one-time opportunity," Mr. Newbridge said.

"Is it possible that this man can also inform me about the men in the truck?" Alex asked.

"I can't tell directly if that is the case. What I can say is that if you ask him and he knows the facts then he will tell you," Mr. Newbridge said and smiled again.

"I understand and thank you for the support in this case. I will be there tomorrow at three pm," Alex said. The men shook hands and Alex left the room.

Alex was full of enthusiasm when he returned to the office. Amanda and Hamid noted the difference in his mood. Alex walked directly to Amanda's desk.

"Hi, Amanda. Please cancel all my after lunch meetings tomorrow. I have another important meeting that I must attend. I think we are going to solve the tattoo mystery at last," Alex said and started to walk into his office when Amanda stopped him.

"Alex. What and where will the meeting tomorrow take place? I need to know."

"Sorry, but I can't tell anybody about it."

"Alex. I must know it's my job and it's about your security also."

"Okay. I understand. I will meet a man at the East Coast Park tomorrow at 3pm. The meeting will take place in Marin Cove. I can't tell you more than that."

"This is all that I need to know. Are you taking anybody with you to that meeting? May I propose Hamid to follow you to that meeting?"

"Sorry to say but I have to go alone. This was a clear message from the Commissioner," Alex said and gave Hamid thumbs up when he passed Hamid's wall of displays.

Ajay was now ready with his hotel report and he walked to Hamid holding a package of papers in his hand.

"Hi, Hamid. Here is my hotel report that you are going to include in the final report of yours," Ajay said and threw the paper package on Hamid's desk.

Hamid was looking at the paper package on his desk and then he looked at Ajay. "Ajay, I want all the reports in digital form and not in analog form. You must have your report on a USB stick," Hamid said.

Ajay did not answer because he was surprised by Hamid's requirement, so he picked up his papers and walked back to his desk in a demonstrative way. Hamid saw that Ajay was upset and angry at his request, so he decided to leave the office. One of Hamid's escape routes was to visit the forensic department and talk to them for a while until most of the heat has cooled down.

———◆———

Chapter

16

The next day, Alex was sitting at the Marin Cove fifteen minutes before 3pm. He was sitting at a table outside and facing the sea. This was his directive that he was given at the Police Commissioner's office.

He was a little bit nervous about this meeting because he did not know how the man looked like. He was looking around the area constantly to identify the person that could be the one that he will meet. He checked the time and now it was precisely 3pm. When he looked up, there was a man standing in front of him. He was a Caucasian man in his sixties and average height, glasses, gray hair and he was wearing a t-shirt and shorts together with jogging shoes. His dialect was not American or Oxford English but more of central European.

"Mr. Alex Hen, I'm here to meet you," Alex stood up and shook the man's hand. The man did present himself as Mr. Frank Wajntraub. "You can call me Frank from now on and I hope I can call you Alex. This is more convenient for both of us," Frank said.

"That's okay for me. We have not met before and I have no idea where you are from and who you represent," Alex said and picked up his notebook to make notes.

"Well, my goal with this meeting is simple. I'm committed to telling you all I know about the tattoos on the dead bodies you have found," Frank said.

"My top Managers have told me that I can trust you in full and I will do that of course," Alex said.

"Those were nice words and I appreciate your straight feedback about my profile," Frank said.

Both men were now sitting silently and looking out over the sea where a lot of vessels were anchored. Both men didn't want to open the discussion straight away. They wanted to know each other more but the situation could not admit it. Alex was focused and stressed to get the information he needed to solve the case. Finally, Alex started to tell the whole story about the two dead men with the tattoos and the information they had. Frank was listening with a lot of concentration.

"Your story confirmed what I have knowledge of. We have seen the tattoos before in other circumstances. I think I need a cup of coffee. Do you need anything?" Frank asked.

"No. I'm okay for now," Alex said, and Frank walked into the coffee shop to buy a cup of coffee. When he returned he started to sip his coffee. Alex could see that Frank was in no hurry to tell him about the tattoos.

"Alex, I will tell you what I know and feel free to ask questions if there is something specific that you want to know," Frank said.

"The North Korean agents' office used the tattoo method for their agents. You know the country is suffering heavily of the international Embargo imposed both from the EU and USA. They are forced to import most of the advanced technical equipment and luxury food items like caviar, wine, and other things. To import all that goods into an international embargo country is not easy. No legitimate company wants to break the international embargo that is imposed against a country. This has severe consequences to their business operation including high fines. So, what do you think they do?" Frank asked Alex.

"They have to establish some type of vessel deliveries to bring all the goods into the country illegally. To use air freight is not an option, I guess," Alex said.

"You are right and those agents in North Korea that are working with the container import business use the tattoos as their ID. Now, the Russian man is coming into the picture. He is the man who bought the material they ask for and arranges the container transport," Frank said sipping his coffee.

"Wow. That was not what I expected. This is the missing link to the two dead men in our case," Alex said, and Frank nodded.

"The Russian man had supplied the North Korean regime for several years through secret container deliveries. We don't know how but now with your findings we know the complete container number. We have not had that before when we were searching for this Russian man's container," Frank said.

"I don't understand why they use tattoos for the container ID?" Alex asked.

"They use the same container the whole time and that was the container that the Russian man had leased for years, under the false name of course. The North Korean agents have the same alphabetic characters on their upper left arm. That was the only way the Russian man could identify the agent. He must deal with different agents every time depending on the cargo that he was delivering. When he checked the tattooed alphabetic number on the agent's arm then he knew that the person was really the right person from North Korea."

"Now I understand why the Russian man has those tattoos. The characters tattooed on the Russian man were also checked by the North Korean agent to identify him," Alex said and smiled when he came to the solution.

"You are starting to see the whole picture now. They never wrote down the complete container ID and never talked about it. That's why it was so difficult to identify," Frank said.

The rain had now stopped and the sun was shining again. The men were sitting in silence watching out over the calm sea. They had no hurry to go anywhere right now. They were only sitting and thinking and enjoying the sea view.

"You have heard what happened to the truck at the port. The whole cabin was blown away by an explosion. We really don't know if it was their own mistake when they adapted it or if it was their intent to explode the bomb when they reached the port gate. The problem I have is that I don't have any idea who those people were and from which country," Alex said.

"My guess is as good as yours. I think we will never know what really happened," Frank said while looking at the sea.

"I really appreciate your information and I must use it for my final report. I hope it's okay for you that I do so?" Alex asked.

"It's okay. I'm here to help you with this but now I also know that you have helped me to identify the container ID that the Russian man has been using for years," Frank said.

Both men were sitting silently and thinking of the next move they need to take individually, and they realized that the meeting was over and there was nothing more to discuss. They shook hands and Frank jogged away into the East Coast Park and Alex drove back to the office.

□□□

Amanda's phone was ringing, and she answered as always. It was from the hospital where Kevin was treated for the gunshot. They called to inform about the good news that Kevin was to be released from the hospital the next day. It would be good if relatives will meet him at the hospital. The sad thing was that the Criminal Investigation Department was the only relative's phone number he had given to the hospital. He had no choice because he did not have any relatives that could be contacted. Amanda confirmed that the relatives will be there to take care of him for the rest of his rehabilitation time.

Amanda was thinking of taking Hamid with her, so she waited until Hamid was back at the office after lunch. She fetched him as soon as he arrived at the office.

"Hamid, I need your help on a mission and I hope you can help me," Amanda said smiling.

"Of course, I will help you; what is it?"

"We are going to pick up Kevin from the hospital tomorrow. Are you okay with that?"

"Great idea to pick him up. Shall we use some of the police cars?"

"No, we have to be more private when we arrive there. I'm also planning to take him directly to the office to meet others as a surprise," she smiled pleased with herself.

□□□

Next day, they left for the hospital and Amanda informed Hamid about the call she received from the hospital. The relatives' phone number that was given to them was the departments. They both felt sad about it.

They reached the hospital and signed all the documents that were needed to have Kevin formally released from the hospital.

"Nice to see you two to pick me up. It feels good to leave this hotel," Kevin said, and they were all laughing to his sarcastic humor.

"We are happy to see you again and we will take you directly to the office. I hope it is okay for you?" Hamid asked, and Kevin nodded.

Kevin was sitting in a wheelchair because he was not allowed to walk and they pushed him directly to the car. He entered the car and sat in the front seat carrying himself from the wheelchair to the seat. When they arrived at the office everybody was applauding him.

"Welcome, Kevin. You have done a remarkable recovery and we are happy to have you back. Well, not today, you still have a couple of days to recover, but soon we hope," Alex said.

"I really want to be back as fast as possible and be the 'Senior Advisor' to Hamid," Kevin said, and they all laughed.

"The rookie is doing fine and now he has the full responsibility to produce the final report of our case also including your sunshine promenade at the port," Ajay said with an explosion of laughing in the office.

"Thank you, all, I feel great to be here," Kevin said and everybody could see that he was touched emotionally by the welcome words.

"Okay, all, let's go back to work," Alex said and Kevin rolled his wheelchair to his desk.

When Alex entered the office, Amanda followed him all the way.

"Alex, I have some good news for you," Amanda said and started to read from the document.

"Good news? I have not heard good news since the last salary increase and that was three years ago," Alex said laughing so loud that the whole office could hear him.

"Alex, your letter from the Police Commissioner," Amanda said and gave the letter to Alex. He read it loudly so Amanda could hear him.

"Case presentation for the Police Commissioner's Committee on June 14." Alex said and continued to read from the letter.

"Mr. Alex Hen. On June 14, you are invited to present the case to the Police Commissioner Committee," I have never done this before Alex said.

"Maybe it's your promotion opportunity," Amanda said smiling but Alex was not amused by the comment.

"Well, we have a couple of days to work with. I have dedicated Hamid already to build a presentation package. I must talk to him about the progress," Alex said and rushed out of the office and walked to Hamid. Hamid was talking to Kevin when Alex reached them.

"Hamid, good news. We have been requested to present the case for the whole Committee on June 14. Can we make it on that day?" Alex asked.

"It's possible but we are still missing some of the pieces to this case," Hamid said with a sad expression on his face.

"What is missing?" Alex asked.

"Well, two important pieces are still missing. One is your report from the meeting with the man at Marin Cove. I have not seen that yet. And the other piece is the identity of those persons in the truck that was blown up. Other than that, we are okay, I think," Hamid said and looked at Kevin who was smiling.

"You are right we need to mobilize all investigation resources to find the facts about the men in the truck. I will take responsibility to finalize my report that's an easy win but the rest needs dedication and speed to get in time," Alex said.

"I will go to the Forensic Department and push them to investigate further what they have," Hamid said and walked out of the office.

Kevin was waving to Amanda that he wanted to get some support. Amanda noticed Kevin's signal and walked to Kevin.

"Amanda, I think I need to go to the supermarket. I must have something for breakfast," Kevin said.

"I will take you home and then the supermarket. First, I must inform Alex that I will leave with you," Amanda said, and she walked into Alex's office to inform him that she was leaving for the day.

———◆———

Chapter

17

When Hamid arrived at the forensic department, he asked around if they had identified the men in the truck. The forensic department boss saw Hamid, so he decided to engage Hamid in the ongoing discussion they had.

"Hamid, welcome and nice to have you here visiting our team. Maybe you can tell us about your view on how we should proceed to search for important information about the men in the truck?" the Forensic Manager asked.

"Think of this work as a research in geography with a simple question to answer. From what geographical location are the persons in the truck coming from?" Hamid said and a lot of the staff was now nodding to Hamid's view with acceptance.

The forensic team started to check the clothes; what fabric, coloring material, and any buttons found. One of the forensic team decided to go for a genetic classification of the body parts. The Forensic Manager was very pleased with Hamid's proposal that really started to get things going forward. Hamid left the forensic team and went back to the office to continue his preparation for the presentation. He saw that Alex was in his room working with something, hopefully with his contribution from the meeting at the Marine Cove.

Hamid was a little nervous about his presentation package, especially now that it was going to be presented at the Commissioner's Committee meeting. It was impossible to know who was going to participate in this meeting, but anyhow it will be his package that will be shown.

❑❑❑

Hamid went to bed and tried to sleep but that was impossible. He was lying in his bed and thinking if there was something missing in his presentation package. Suddenly, he realized that one of the most important facts was missing and that was the men's motivation to do this. Hamid looked at his watch beside the bed and it showed half past two. He was clearly awake and highly concerned about the men's motivation and goal with their operation. This question was hunting Hamid the whole night. He was in a desperate need to get an answer on this in his report. Why did they really want to steal the container and end their lives in the port? Some strong motivation should have been in the background to do this. He was convinced that the knowledge of this motivation would be good to know for the future. He started to think about who could deliver the right hypothesis on this. He had to discuss this with Alex first thing the next morning.

The next morning, Hamid walked into Alex's office to discuss the report package. Alex was ready with this report from Marin Cove and handed over the USB stick where he had stored his report.

"Thank you. This is great to have everything stored in this stick," Hamid said.

"You should not expect anything else from me. I'm a modern man and I use the technology," Alex said with a smile.

"We have now all the facts about the case in this USB stick," Hamid said and showed over fifty pages of material to Alex. He had also included the facts that the container was not damaged by the explosion only rolled backward a couple of meters. The front of the container was black because of the fire, but the content was not damaged as they could see. Firefighters at the port were fast to pour a lot of water on it to cool it down. The container had gone through a structural check and it was approved for shipping use.

"I had also contacted the Army to check if they have anything new to say. They told me that the ammunition and automatic machine guns have different country of origin. The conclusion was that it was not any specific country that had supplied the terrorists with heavy weapons. It was more of a pick and pack material from different countries with different quality. The same was for the ammunition produced by several different countries. The bomb attached to one of the crane legs was also analyzed but nothing specific; ordinary TNT was used," Hamid said and presented his package so far on the screen for Alex to see.

"Wow, I'm impressed that we have so many facts about the case. You have much more than I expected. Is this all or are we missing something?" Alex asked.

Hamid was silent for a while before he started to talk about his concerns.

"Well, Alex, how shall I put it? We don't have the motive why these men in the truck wanted to grab the container and what was the purpose. I have been thinking about this a lot, but I don't have any answers and I don't know who can answer these questions. The question is also, whether we should put this part into our presentation or not," Hamid said.

"You are right. Let's think about it, but I don't know if we shall take this into our package. We are representing the Criminal Investigation Department and that means we stay strictly to the facts we have found. However, if there is an expressed demand from the Police Commissioner's Committee to have a hypothesis on the case. Well, we can request somebody to present that," Alex said in a convincing voice.

"We need to secure this if the Committee asked about it and in fact, I think they will. I will make the whole presentation ready today and bring it to you on a USB stick," Hamid said and started to walk out from the room.

"Hamid, stop, I have something more for you. I want you to finalize the container transport to Rotterdam as planned. You know the routines already, how to do it. Can you also arrange someone to clean it from outside? I saw it on the TV and it looked black because of smoke and dust."

"Okay, I will get it done," Hamid said.

"And I will talk to the Commissioner if she can help us to invite someone to present this," Alex said.

◻◻◻

Later the same day, Hamid delivered the presentation package to Alex on a USB stick as he had promised. Alex started to walk through the presentation. He was measuring the total time of the presentation and reviewed the text to all pictures. This was his chance to make an impression to the Committee members. He decided to call Catherine about his concerns on how to handle the terrorists in the truck. Catherine answered when she saw that it was Alex calling.

"Hi, Alex. Working with the presentation, I guess," Catherine said.

"You are right. I have a problem and that is we have nothing to say about those persons in the truck. There is nothing to present and I don't want to speculate. How shall we handle that if the Committee has questions?" Alex asked and continued.

"The other thing is that we don't know the terrorist's intention with the container content. I think it's not my work to present the hypothetical ideas around the terrorists. My job is to present hard facts and nothing more," Alex said.

"You are right so let's have it in that way. I will arrange someone else to present the hypothetical scenarios related to the terrorists."

"This is a big relief for me. May I ask how you are going to solve this part of the presentation?" Alex asked.

"I have an idea for this. I will first discuss this with the Chairman. It will be a surprise for all members at the meeting. I will make sure that you will have the opportunity to participate and listen to this person." Catherine said.

"I understand that will be interesting. See you at the meeting tomorrow." Alex said as they both ended the call.

Everything was now ready for the closing report and Alex was dedicated to his task.

———◆———

PART EIGHT

The Closing Report

Chapter

18

The Commissioners' Committee was now gathered with all the ordinary members and specially invited guests. The Committee's Chairman opened the meeting as usual.

"Members, welcome to this meeting. It is going to be the case closing meeting of the container incident. You can see that we have invited guests from several Government departments. They have, of course, helped in their capacity in the case and the closing information will be shown here. I will not introduce everyone in person since you have had the opportunity to meet them at the lobby. The Army and its operations will be represented by General Mr. Tong and he has been in this meeting before," the Chairman said and nodded to Catherine to get ready for her side of the presentation.

Catherine started the overhead projector before the Chairman announced the first presenter and that was as usual Catherine.

"Catherine will be starting with the general presentation of the case so that the guests can have an understanding of what has happened and where we are," Chairman said.

"Thank you, Mr. Chairman. This case has been a very difficult and unusual one for us at the Police force. We have stretched all our capabilities to the maximum; in manpower and also in our competence to solve this case. One of the things that I wanted to say is that we have been fortunate to have support from colleagues and other international crime-fighting organizations," Catherine took a pause in her speech and looked around the table. Most members were nodding to confirm her words. She continued. "This time, I will not do the actual presentation. I have, instead, invited the Head of Criminal Investigation Department, Mr. Alex Hen."

Catherine's secretary opened the conference room door and Alex walked in. Catherine showed Alex the place he was to sit during the meeting. Alex connected the HDMI cord to his laptop and Hamid's presentation package was now projecting on the screen.

The first title slide with Hamid's name was 'The Container Incident' Report. Alex started his presentation.

"Committee members, my name is Alex Hen and I'm the Head of Criminal Investigation Department. This presentation is going to be on the facts we have found." Alex said and was looking at the members. Alex presented the slides one by one and talked about the facts on each of them. He showed the two dead men, tattoos on the upper left arm, container ID, North Korea, false passport, Chinese vessel, Russian dealer, container content, intercontinental missiles, nuclear warheads, returning the container to Rotterdam, Kevin shot, container hijacked, army execution, port occupation, crane blowing up, explosion at the gate, hotel findings, terrorist group, citizenship unknown, no demands, unknown purpose to take the container. Alex presentation was ready after fifty-five slides.

"This was all; however, there is, of course, a more detailed written report of the case according to our normal procedures," Alex said and closed his laptop.

Catherine was smiling at Alex and looked pleased by his presentation. The Chairman smiled also and nodded to confirm that he too liked what Alex had presented. The Chairman stood up and started to talk again.

"Members, after this excellent presentation by Mr. Hen, I propose we take a break before we continue," the Chairman said, and all members agreed to the proposal by standing up.

During the break, several of the Commissioner's Committee members approached Alex and asked him some specific questions regarding the presentation. The representatives from the Government asked questions that were relevant to their area of responsibility. Alex could answer most of the questions and everybody expressed their appreciation for his presentation.

Commissioner's secretary requested the members to return to the session otherwise they might end up outside talking for hours. She succeeded with this task and well in time. All members had gathered again in the conference room. Alex could also stay in the conference room and listen to the unknown presenter. The Chairman talked again and introduced the next person.

"Members, I have on request by Catherine, decided to call in a person from the Internal Security Department specialized in terrorist groups. Mr. Naveen Anand. He has been studying this case closely and of course, he has full access to the investigation results," the Chairman said, and Catherine's secretary opened the conference door and Mr. Anand entered the room. He was a well-dressed man around forty-something years of age, was of Indian origin and taller than average.

"Committee members, thank you for the invitation as this is my first presentation for this Committee. I'm glad to be here and talk about the scenario that we think can finally close this case. I have no overhead package to present to you. I will talk to you directly instead if that's okay with you?" Mr. Anand asked, and the members nodded in acceptance.

"The terrorists that were in the truck were from different geographical areas, but we don't know from which specific countries. There is no information found in any communication media that can give us an indication about where they met and what they planned. Based on the DNA characteristics we can place them in Africa, the Middle East, Europe, and Asia. There were no more facts found as Mr. Hen has presented to you. However, we have our scenario that we think is close to the facts," Mr. Anand said and started to walk around in the conference room. He took a pause for thought before he started to talk. "A scenario can be seen as the truth specifically if the press can get hold of it."

Mr. Anand walked around in the conference room and then he continued. "A scenario is always coming into play when facts are missing or unclear like now with the terrorists in the truck," Anand said and looked at the Committee members and the Chairman. The Chairman nodded to support his words and Mr. Anand continued his scenario presentation.

"This is our scenario. This group in the truck is representing a new type of terrorist groups with international members. They don't have any specific religious faith that gives followers the financial support to initiate terrorist actions. They are well educated and technically competent young people. They have now proven this capability by knowing exactly where the container was placed in the port. The surprising thing was also that they had the knowledge of the day when it was planned to be loaded on the vessel. They have a common political agenda that holds them together and nothing else. We think, they belong to the newly formed left-wing militant organization with the goal to create chaos and fear in the society through terrorist actions. The terrorist actions will provide them an opportunity to take over the political agenda for the targeted country. If you remember the European terrorist groups like the Baader-Meinhof group, Action Direct, and others. Those groups were active in the early and late 1970s. Our main scenario is that we think this group has the same type of agenda as those groups. The people in the truck belong to a newly created similar organization totally unknown to us and our allied countries. Any questions?" Mr. Anand asked but everybody was silent, so he continued, "If this is a new terrorist organization, with this type of capabilities and love for destruction, then they will be difficult to find and control. Everything points us to the belief that the group in the truck was the first active cell in this new terrorist organization and they have the motivation to initiate more such actions. Any questions?"

"What do you think was their purpose to take the container and for what use do you think they wanted to use it?" one member asked.

"It's hard to say but it was an advanced plan that almost worked. I can guess that their plan was to sell it to the highest bidder to finance their terrorist activities or to create a devastating bomb. We should be happy that their plan was stopped by our Police force." Mr. Anand said.

"Do you think there are more such terrorist cells in Asia?" an old member asked who was representing the Foreign Ministry.

"Sorry to say, but we really don't know. We don't really have any communication traces which may point to that direction. It's possible because we don't know who stole the truck in Malaysia. And how many more such missions are planned," Mr. Anand said.

"But we have to know. This is a very dangerous development," another member said.

"I agree, and we are working on it. With those words, I should end my scenario walk through," Mr. Anand said with a smile and he walked to the side wall to sit down beside Alex.

Everyone was silent in the conference room and it was obvious that all members were shocked by the scenario that was presented. The Chairman was looking around the table if any member wanted to say or ask something, but nobody wanted to talk right now.

"I think that Mr. Anand's scenario presentation has touched us all. We must remember that this is a scenario and not the facts. But we must be prepared to face the scenario in reality. Any questions?"

"Where is the container now and what's the plan? What I understand is that it's still at the port," one member asked.

"I think that Mr. Hen or the General shall answer that question. After all, the Army is still responsible for the port area," the Chairman said.

The General did not stand up to talk this time. In his opinion, the question was more directed to Alex. So, he remained seated and spoke briefly. "The situation is like this. The Army has now, as we speak, armed guards watching over the container round the clock. Alex, can you tell something more?"

"My personnel at the Criminal Investigation Department have now reserved space on the vessel for the container to be transported to Rotterdam according to the previous plan by the Committee. It has also been cleaned off the burning debris and marks and repainted on damaged areas. We want it to look nice for the European authorities when they receive," Alex said, and everybody was laughing. Even the General smiled a little.

"I will go to the port after this meeting to see it myself when it will be loaded onboard for the transport. Do you want to follow with me?" Alex asked the General.

"Absolutely, I would want to see this when it happens," the General said, and all were laughing again.

The Chairman decided to close the meeting, so he stood up and started to speak.

"Committee members and guests, I think we have a common understanding about this case and the facts around it. Our Police force has worked hard to collect all the facts and solved several difficult challenges like resources, material, and competence. Our Army has of course taken their responsibility fully by exposing their men to real danger; almost like a war zone. I think you all agree with me when I thank the Police force and the Army for a well-performed work for our nation. We also understand the possible scenario that might develop in the future described by Mr. Anand. With these words, I close this meeting," the chairman said and there was an applause in the room as that had never happened before.

The Committee meeting was over, and the members walked slowly out of the conference room talking about the meeting and the presentations. Catherine walked to Alex to thank him for his presentation.

"Alex, thank you. I'm proud of you for how you handled this critical case and now this presentation. You and your men have performed the best all the time. I have, however, one more demand that I want you to fulfill," Catherine said when they walked out of the conference room.

Alex stopped walking and looked at Catherine with serious eyes.

"I hope I can fulfill it. Tell me what it is?"

"I want you to take Kevin and Hamid with you to the port. They must see when the container is loaded on the vessel," Catherine said.

"You are right and that is a very good idea."

□□□

Alex walked into the office with fast steps showing his happiness very well. He saw Kevin without the wheelchair and Hamid in the coffee area, so he walked in there directly. He passed Amanda's desk without saying anything. Amanda looked up surprisingly as she was used to the fact that Alex always said something to her while passing her desk but not this time. So, she followed Alex into the coffee area.

"Kevin and Hamid, I have some good news for you," Kevin said and pushed some buttons for coffee.

"It looks like you have been promoted at the Commissioner's meeting," Amanda said, and they all laughed.

"Why would you think that?" Alex asked Amanda.

"Well, usually when you come into the office, you say something about the weather, traffic or your morning meetings. But today, you just walked by my desk without a word."

"You must be occupied because you were thinking about your new paycheck," Kevin said and they all laughed.

"Sorry. Sorry. I'm so excited about the meeting with the Committee. It was scary and interesting at the same time. Everything went well with all the case facts that we have collected," Alex said sipping his coffee.

"I have worked closely with the Army logistics contingent to arrange everything so that the container can be shipped safely to Rotterdam," Hamid said.

"Great. You, Hamid, have done this planning very well and you did well in making that presentation," Alex said.

"Thank you. The container is ready for shipping tonight," Hamid said.

"You know what?" Alex said and was looking at them both.

Both Kevin and Hamid were waiting for his answer, but Alex was really enjoying exploiting their curiosity before answering.

"Both of you are going with me to the port together with the General to see live when the container is loaded. We are going there with the General's armored vehicle. Are you ready for this experience?" Alex asked and they both showed their thumbs to accept the offer.

"That will be a fantastic closing of this case and you are both worth it," Amanda said.

Alex's mobile rang and it was the General. He was now parked outside the Criminal Investigation Department's office. Alex answered.

"Yes. Hi. Both Kevin and Hamid will go with us to the port and they are ready," Alex said and hung up the phone.

"Gentlemen, we need to go down to the main gate as the General is waiting for us," Alex said.

□□□

They entered the General's armored vehicle and they shook hands with the General. The armored vehicle was not going very fast on the highway, but the traffic gave them space when they drove through. The seats were not comfortable and the view to the outside was very limited. They seem to be relieved when they exited the vehicle to meet the Port Master.

His injuries were mainly caused by flying glass debris when the explosion crashed the window where he was standing and looking out. He had some scars on his face from the explosion but nothing more was visible.

"Gentlemen, welcome to the port again. I must say that you entered in style this time and well protected in an armored vehicle. After what happened, I am thinking of buying one too," the Port Master said, and everybody laughed.

"Yes, high security is the word of the day. We want to see the live loading of the container. I have brought with me key people from my department who had been involved in this case," Alex said.

"Yes, I can recognize Kevin and Hamid," the Port Master said.

Then the general exited the armored vehicle and he saluted the Port Master and the Port Master did the same.

"General, good to see you here again. Your men have guarded the container round the clock, and we are happy to have you here," the Port Master said.

"Good to hear. Shall we enter the vehicle and roll into the port? You can come with us in this vehicle," the General said and jumped into the armored vehicle together with all the others.

❏❏❏

There were four armored Army vehicles parked around the container. The General jumped out of the vehicle and saluted the soldiers that were standing in front of their vehicles. The General conducted a brief inspection of the soldiers' and then he held a short thanks speech to them. The container was placed close to the crane to have it in full sight all the time and easy to load. The Port Master had to notify the others that the crane was now moving and going to load the container.

"Gentlemen, can I have your attention? The container will now be loaded on the vessel," the General said, and all eyes were now on the crane and the container.

The container was now hanging under the crane and slowly moving above the vessel and then lowered down on the vessel.

The General saluted to Alex and he did the same and they shook hands over a mission accomplished. This was also the formal handover of the port responsibility from the Army to the Police force.

"There it goes our SCNU3604628 and I'm glad to see it on its way," Hamid said looking at the container.

"Hopefully, we will not get a similar case in the future that can ruin my retirement," Kevin said, and everybody laughed again.

"We have handled this container incident very professionally," Alex said.

"The newly formed terrorist cell has now been destroyed before it could expand," the General said, and they all nodded.

The newly formed Asian terrorist cell was destroyed for now. But are more of its members hiding in sleeping cells? Only time will tell if that was the case.

———◆———